PENGUIN BOOKS

IN A DARK ROOM WITH A STRANGER

Brian McCabe was born in a small mining community near Edinburgh. Since 1980 he has lived as a freelance writer. He has published two volumes of poetry, *Spring's Witch* (1984) and *One Atom to Another* (1987), and a collection of short stories entitled *The Lipstick Circus* (1985). His highly acclaimed novel, *The Other McCoy*, (1990) is also published by Penguin. He lives with his family in Edinburgh.

BRIAN McCABE

IN A DARK ROOM WITH A STRANGER

PENGUIN BOOKS

For my sister Valerie

PENGUIN BOOKS

Published by the Penguin Group
Penguin Books Ltd, 27 Wrights Lane, London W8 5TZ, England
Penguin Books USA Inc., 375 Hudson Street, New York, New York 10014, USA
Penguin Books Australia Ltd, Ringwood, Victoria, Australia
Penguin Books Canada Ltd, 10 Alcorn Avenue, Toronto, Ontario, Canada M4V 3B2
Penguin Books (NZ) Ltd, 182–190 Wairau Road, Auckland 10, New Zealand

Penguin Books Ltd, Registered Offices: Harmondsworth, Middlesex, England

First published by Hamish Hamilton 1993
Published in Penguin Books 1995
1 3 5 7 9 10 8 6 4 2

Printed in England by Clays Ltd, St Ives plc

Contents

Acknowledgements

Some of these stories have previously appeared in: *Best Short Stories 1992* (Heinemann, 1992); *I can sing, dance, rollerskate* (HarperCollins, 1988); the *Malahat Review* (Vancouver); *Pig Squealing* (A.S.L.S., 1992); *Radical Scotland*; *The Red Hog of Colima* (HarperCollins, 1989); *Scotland on Sunday*; the *Scotsman*; *Scottish Short Stories 1993* (HarperCollins).

'A Good Night's Sleep' and 'Kreativ Riting' were first broadcast by BBC Radio 4's *Morning Story*. An earlier version of 'Say Something' was broadcast by BBC Radio 3.

The author would like to thank the Scottish Arts Council for a bursary, and the Hawthornden Foundation for a one-month fellowship, both of which gave him time to complete this collection.

Strange Passenger

Going home always felt worse than leaving. The train hadn't changed in all the years I'd been taking it: the same stops at stations where no one seemed to get on or off; the same unexplained delays, blocked toilets and litter-strewn carriages with worn seats. It was always either empty and freezing or, like today, overcrowded and stifling. It was a sultry afternoon. I hadn't slept after my eldest sister Angela had called to tell me the news about Dad. She'd been called into the hospital after midnight and had sat with him. She'd left the room for a few minutes and when she'd gone back, 'he was *very dead*'. Somehow the phrase was much more specific than just 'dead'. She'd seen something I hadn't, something I couldn't quite imagine: our father being very dead.

My reaction had been – but had there been any real reaction? Hadn't I just made the sorrowful and shocked noises appropriate to the occasion?

Then I'd gone back into the bedroom to tell Polly. Her reaction was more dramatic, and it embarrassed me: tears sprang into her eyes – maybe my father's death reminded her of the death of her own father? Or maybe her emotions were riding high in any case. Before the call, we'd been building up to an argument all evening. She'd first mentioned that her period was late a few days ago and it had come up again tonight, after the spaghetti bolognese and the bottle of cheap red wine. This time she'd wanted to talk about exactly what we were going to do if she was, and my unwillingness to discuss it had made her angry and tearful. She'd demanded to know how I felt about it, but I'd been coolly evasive, treating the whole thing like a hypothetical ethical dilemma from Moral Phil. 1.

After the call, of course, I'd had the perfect excuse to drop the whole question of the pregnancy: my father's death. So, although she'd held her arms out to me I hadn't gone to her. Instead I'd told her I wanted to be on my own for a while and had gone to sit in the kitchen. I'd sat there for a long time, trying in vain to realize what had happened, trying to find the reaction in myself I knew should be there, but I'd found nothing except a vague numbness, an inability to feel. The more I'd tried to focus my mind on it, the more remote and abstract it had seemed. Of course, I was a final-year student of Philosophy, so maybe everything had become a bit remote and abstract. I'd tried to think of my father in his life, of the good and fond memories of him I undoubtedly had, but even this proved to be impossible. The recent image of him as he lay dying in hospital, paralysed down one side of his body and having lost the power of speech, obliterated the others. Added to this was a sense of anti-climax the death brought with it: he'd been dying for a long time, all the family knew it, and it was difficult to feel anything like shock.

So I'd sat up through the night, smoking my thin, hand-rolled cigarettes, trying to feel something real about my father and experiencing only an uncomfortable awareness of myself – of my own physical movements as I sat there smoking, but also the movements of my thoughts, such as they were. I wasn't really in my thoughts, but apart from them, like some-one reading about himself in his own diary. Could this be how grief started, I wondered – as a kind of dissociation, a kind of absence of feeling? Maybe Nietzsche, the unwilling subject of my unfinished and, I suspected, unfinishable dissertation, had written an aphorism about it somewhere, but if so I couldn't remember in which book, or what it said. Wouldn't he equate grief with guilt, and thence the life-denying instinct of the herd? Anyway, although I was half-buried in my footnotes to *Beyond Good and Evil*, I was beginning to have doubts about academia: hadn't my father once said to me that you shouldn't have to look up a book to know what you think? Didn't that apply even more to what you felt?

And wasn't Nietzsche partly to blame for the way I was acting about Polly? I'd been living with her for two years, but still didn't feel quite committed to her. The idea that she might be pregnant made me feel less so. Nietzsche encouraged me to give the V-sign to commitment when it suited me. I mean, would the Overman, who was capable of creating his own moral values, worry about such things? Of course he wouldn't. There were no absolutes. Anything was permissible. Nothing was taboo.

I'd gone back to bed briefly that morning, but hadn't been able to sleep. Then Angela had called up again to tell me about the arrangements. The body would be transferred to Agnew's, the undertaker's in Murkirk, that morning. The funeral would be in two days' time.

There was this persistent, pulsating ache behind my temples. My hands were clammy and swollen and I'd bitten my fingernails to the quick. My shirt adhered to my back like a membrane, a second skin I longed to shed. I shuddered despite the heat. I was bothered by the nearness of the other passengers, especially the two who sat on either side of me. That asthmatic old lady on my left was the last thing I needed. She kept wheezing and muttering under her breath, and her sickly perfume hung in the air like a premonition of something rotten. The dumpy, crew-cutted teenage boy on my right was just as bad. He kept crunching his crisps noisily and jiggling his thigh up and down on the seat to the demented beat of the heavy-metal music on his pocket radio.

I felt like tapping him on the shoulder and saying:

'D'you mind? I'm in mourning.'

But no, that would be melodramatic, another way of falsifying what I felt, if I felt anything. For the moment, I felt only the intense discomfort of the journey. I rearranged myself in the seat, trying to make more room for my legs and my elbows between the two on either side of me. On the seat opposite there was a young couple with a crying baby. The mother was harassed, the father sullen. The baby kept crying and being sick, and they kept having to search in their several bags, which were crammed together on the floor between us, for bottles and tissues and baby-wipes. I couldn't imagine me and Polly with a baby. I didn't want to.

I watched the baby opposite kicking its legs and drumming its chubby fists in the air. Its screwed-up face seemed to swell and redden, as if about to burst, every time it drew breath to cry. It looked to me like anger itself as it cried as hard as it could cry. The mother was rocking it furiously, but I could see she was too much on edge, at the end of her tether with it. Then the father held his hands out to take the baby and the mother sighed with exasperation and passed it over to him. He held the baby close to his face, so that his nose came into contact with its head – he was *breathing* on it! Then *he* began to rock, slowly, backwards and forwards, and as he did he murmured something to the baby, or maybe he was humming a tune to it. He looked almost as if he was dancing, from the waist up, slowly, as if he was remembering being at the dancing and it was a slow slushy number, like 'Please release me, let me go . . . ' It was working. The baby's cries lessened and soon it fell asleep.

Could I have done that? I wondered, and stared with a kind of appalled admiration at the father. Christ, he was a young guy, about the same age as me, probably younger, but he looked older, unshaven and exhausted, his unkempt black hair drooping over one eye. He wore a nylon, short-sleeved, open-necked shirt printed with the kind of pattern you sometimes saw on tumblers, made up of intersecting circles and triangles and lines.

He went on rocking, humming and staring into space, as if he was still at the dancing, then he noticed that I was watching him, flicked the hair out of his eye and smiled at me, and his smile seemed to say it all. Look at me, the smile seemed to say, look and be warned: this could be you, pal. I smiled back uncertainly, nodding my head at the baby. I wanted to say something, but I didn't know what to say. Well done? That seems to have done the trick?

The wheezing old lady beat me to it, but she spoke to the mother:

'Ah doubt she's gonnae be a daddy's girl! What's her name?'

'Tracy.'

The old woman wheezed and said it was a lovely name.

Jesus Christ, if Polly was pregnant, she might want to have the baby. Not that we'd discussed it properly last night, but now it seemed to me that she'd been less against the idea than she should be. Maybe that was because she knew she wasn't, but maybe not, maybe she knew by intuition that she was and felt OK about it, even if it would mess up her last year at the art college. There was no accounting for what hormones could do.

What would we call it – Kandinsky or Zarathustra?

The light, which had a steely glare, was hurting my eyes. I tried shutting them, but then the pounding in my head seemed to louden, jarred to a crescendo by the thud of the carriage door every time it slid open and shut as the slow train rumbled and lurched along the track, which needed to be relaid, to Murkirk.

When my restlessness became insufferable, I stood up and walked to the next carriage, which was just as crowded as the last and just as airless. One or two of the passengers eyed me as I moved up the train, but without curiosity – if anything they looked furtive and threatened.

Was I just imagining it, the hostility and the defeat in their eyes, or was it there to be seen, almost a public statement, deliberate and unanimous? Or was it just that I was seeing things strangely today – because my father had died, or because I hadn't slept, or because I had a head full of *The Anti-Christ*?

The herd. They were what Nietzsche called the herd, and I moved among them as an outsider, a strange passenger. When I came to the front of the train I found a free window in the corridor where no one was standing. I tried to open it, but it was jammed shut. I leaned against it and, shielding my eyes from the sun with a hand, peered out through the glass – almost opaque with grime from the train's endless journey through the Central Belt. The first thing I saw was, around a squat black church with a mean little spire, the huddled stones of a village graveyard. Even then, I had to prod my own mind to make the connection this should have had with death.

It was the same landscape I'd seen so many times from the train, industrial, with short stretches of what could be called countryside in between, but these were so featureless and haphazard that they seemed like brief interludes in the interminable story of the factories, the warehouses, the car parks and the housing schemes ... The backs of those drab brown houses, with their coal bunkers and their drying greens and their kitchen windows, looked like stunted, blighted faces.

The same landscape, but something about it was changing,

and it was like the change was taking place right there before my eyes: a boarded-up building that had been a working factory, I was sure, the last time I'd seen it; a corner of wasteground where a school had been demolished but nothing had been built; a shop up for sale; a vandalized bus shelter; a gang of teenagers sitting on a wall. Unemployment had stamped on the faces of these small towns and villages, leaving them with broken teeth and empty eyes, and it would stamp on them again.

My education had taken me away, but one day I might have to return – to work in a school here, teaching kids how to pass exams and get out, or fail exams and stay and be forgotten except as statistics in the unemployment figures. I might have to work here where others wouldn't find work, because I might have to be a teacher – what else could I do? If Polly was pregnant, and if she went ahead and had the baby – Christ! I'd have to do something for money. On the other hand, she might be late. She'd been later than this before.

I turned from the window and started to make my way up the train, because it was slowing down as it neared the station, and already I was surrounded by it, the herd of shuffling, muttering Murkirk folk. They sounded resigned to having arrived at their destination.

The funeral parlour was modern. I had not expected this, especially in Murkirk. The plate glass doors, the expansive foyer furnished with maroon leather chairs and mahogany wood-panelling – all of it smacked of a business venture whose success had proved to be beyond the scope of its founder's most outrageous dreams.

I crossed the foyer to the reception desk. I looked through the glass at a woman who sat there typing something. She was in her late thirties, but there was something older about her.

Her dress, for one thing, belonged to the late fifties or early sixties, the time of bouffant hairdos, heavy eye make-up and twin-sets and pearls. And she wore these winged glasses, almost like the kind my mother wore, and they made her big brown eyes look like dead leaves stuck to a window pane.

'Can I help you?'

For some reason I wanted to shock her.

'I've come to see my old man.'

She ignored the casualness of this and asked me for the name, opened a desk diary and ran a manicured talon down a column.

'D'you have an appointment?'

'No.'

She admonished me briefly over the specs.

'It didn't occur to me that he'd be busy.'

That hit the target all right. She wasn't amused. She wasn't shocked either, but she gave me a quick, hard look, a look I'd seen before, full of a kind of hostile curiosity. It was the look of those who'd never left Murkirk and never would, never step outside their lives and look in. It was the look, I decided, of the herd.

'I'll just see if Mr Agnew can make arrangements, if you'd like to take a seat.'

I decided to make myself plain, so I bleated at her before walking away to the waiting area. She looked at me steadily as I uttered the bleat, but I knew it was hopeless. Already she had me pigeon-holed as a drug addict or a weirdo.

I resented having to wait. I resented the place, with its ugly, fake-antique furniture. Wasn't this coffee table, with its pile of magazines, the limit?

Who'd want to read a magazine while waiting to visit their dead? But apparently people did, because here they were. I picked one up and opened it to see a picture of a mother holding a towel to the cheek of her baby's face. The baby was smiling, his or her bright blue eyes gleaming with glee, the rosy cheeks shining with health and vigour. The mother was smiling too, a caring, reassuring smile at the baby. It was an advertisement for fabric softener, but to me it was another reminder. Christ, I wasn't ready for it. My own father had just died, I wasn't ready to step into those shoes.

Mr Agnew was not what I'd expected an undertaker to be. He hurried from a door at the rear of the reception area and stuck on a smile for me as he approached, extending a clean – the word I thought of was 'pampered' – hand. A strange thought shot through my mind as I shook the hand – that maybe he washed his hands before handling a corpse as well as after, as if afraid that the living might contaminate the dead. A whiff of after-shave – or was it something else? – accompanied a business-like manner as the face of Mr Agnew came too close for comfort.

It was not an undertaker's face. No solemn, sunken eyes or deathly pallor. Nothing sepulchral. No mournful moustache framing a bejowled, doom-heavy mouth. He looked, if anything, obscenely healthy, with the ruddy complexion of those who eat well and get plenty of fresh air. He explained that because I hadn't made an appointment, it would take a few minutes to make the necessary arrangements so that I could see my father. His demeanour was irrepressibly that of the businessman. It wasn't just the pin-striped suit and the brisk manner. It was also the way he narrowed his eyes when he looked at me, as if sizing up a cadaver of the future. True, there were other gestures and mannerisms more suited to his profession: a restrained tone of voice as he spoke, a certain inclination of the head acquired by the habit of commiseration, but these did little to disguise the manner of man he was. As he walked away, I thought I sensed something amiss with him, some discomfort, as if he hadn't found time for something or had forgotten to put something on his agenda, like clipping his toenails. Maybe attending to the minor needs of so many other bodies made him neglect the demands of his own? It was the way he walked that made me think of this – it looked like it pained his feet to come into contact with the floor. Maybe his shoes were just a bit too tight.

I waited again.

I tried to remember something about my father, something that would suit the dignity of the occasion, but what came into my mind wasn't dignified – it happened on a weekend visit home.

When I come into the house, they are in the kitchen. My father is sitting at the formica-topped kitchen table, reading the *Murkirk Gazette*, while my mother finishes off making the tea. After the usual greetings, my father says to me:

'Where the hell's fire have you been?'

I smile. It's what he always says when I come home.

'That's where I've been.'

My dad laughs and cries out:

'Hear that, Mary? Says he's been tae hell! He's met the devil hissel!'

My mother is too busy laying out the food on the plates to pay any attention.

She puts my plate down on the table in front of me. There is protein there and carbohydrate, and as a concession to fresh vegetables a fried tomato dominates the colour-scheme of the platter, alongside which, on the table, she puts two slices of plain white bread, liberally margarined, and a cup of strong, heavily sugared tea.

'Tae hell and back! D'ye hear that, Mary?'

My mother, confused by this loose talk of hell and wary of

my father's moods – even when they are good, she knows how quickly they can change – ignores him and says to me:

'Ye'll enjoy that, son.'

'He hasnae ate a meal since he was last hame. Look at him, skinny izza rake! Play a tune on his ribs! Is that aw ye're gien him?'

My mother tuts agitatedly.

I am beginning to feel some indefinable discomfort I've often felt when my father jests with my mother like this. I look at the mixed grill in front of me and say:

'I'll never eat all this, Mum.'

'You will so.'

I half expect her to add that I'm a growing laddie, but she doesn't. Still, there's a hint of command in her scandalized tone of voice. Maybe she has always made me do what she wants me to, not by being strict, but by the opposite stratagem – by indulging me in her love. Maybe in the very act of giving, of providing, she makes me feel obliged to her. Anyway, I know that anything left on the plate will be in the nature of a filial insult, a criticism of her personally.

'Is that aw he's gettin for his tea?' my dad exclaims, running a hard palm over his bald, pitted scalp and shaking his head in mock disbelief.

My mother adjusts her glasses, which magnify her eyes to make them look permanently affronted, takes her hanky from her sleeve, sniffs into it and glares at him, daring him to go on.

'I thought ye'd have killed thon fatted calf, Mary.'

She raises her eyebrows, and executes a kind of little mime show, closing her eyes and spreading a hand over her chest, as if about to faint. When she laughs, it is forced and shrill, like the cry of a panicking bird. My father's humour always makes her think of things she'd rather not think about. His jokes are tainted with politics or religion and they never cease to put her on edge.

'Did ye no defrost thon fatted calf in the freezer? Ah mean, the boy's been tae hell and back and he comes hame, the Prodigal returns, expectin a fatted calf, at least wan, tae be slaughtered for him . . .'

'Aw, stop it – please!'

She tries to change the subject:

'Are ye enjoying your tea, son?'

Here I echo my father:

'It's the first decent meal I've had since I was last here, Mum.'

'It is not!'

She is frowning and smiling at the same time. The idea is as pleasing as it is scandalous.

'I'm sure Polly feeds you well,' she adds, sceptically.

'It's no the same as his Mammy's, eh no son?'

I nod and smile and try not to show that I'm having trouble with the black pudding. The egg, the greyish sausages, the tattie scones, the fried tomato and the greasy, fatty bacon are going down OK, but I'm definitely having trouble with the black pudding, which is soggy in the middle and partially uncooked. To make matters worse, I remember my father telling me off as a boy for not eating my black pudding at Sunday Breakfast.

'Shovel it doon yer gullet!' had been his exact words then.

As if reading my thoughts, he gives me a penetrating look and says the same thing now:

'Shovel it doon yer gullet!'

My mother looks worriedly at all the food I've still to eat.

'Finish your tea, son. There's more black puddin if ye want it.'

'There's a fatted calf in the freezer there,' says my father.

My mother closes her eyes, holds her hands up in a parody of despair and exhorts:

'Aw please, don't!'

I raise a clot of the dried blood to my lips. I know my mother is watching me and waiting. I'm beginning to feel queasy, and when I take a mouthful of the grisly black pudding, I taste the metal of the fork – it's a worn fork that has lost its shine and gone grey. The metallic taste of the fork lingers in my mouth and I feel nauseous.

It's now that it happens:

My dad, playing the fool, reaches over to filch a sausage from my plate.

'Gi'us a wee bitty that fatted calf, Prodigal!'

My reaction is instinctive, almost a reflex – it's not that I desperately want to keep the sausage. It's his mischievousness I'm reacting to. Maybe I'm just not in the mood for it and he senses this and does it all the more to tease me. Anyway, I raise my fist in a warning gesture. But, and this is the strange thing, somehow the clenched fist takes on a life of its own, all restraint dissolves and, without meaning to, I punch him so hard on the arm that he drops his fork and recoils in pain. He screws up his face and bellows in outrage.

My mother's mouth falls open in horror, and I suppose that my own mouth does something similar, because I am truly astonished at what I have done: I have hit my father, hit him hard, I have hurt him. Then I see the anger flaring in his piercing blue eyes and I know I have to run. And I do run, and with good reason, because my father is chasing me through the house, shouting and cursing. And here is another curious thing: although I'm scared of what he might do to me if he catches me, I'm also laughing hysterically. I glance over my shoulder as he chases me up the stairs, and the sight of his enraged, inflamed face makes me giggle all the more. I am still giggling as I shut and lock the bathroom door on him, and the sound of his fists beating on the door, and the sight of the door shuddering with the violence of his fury – all of it only makes me laugh all the more uncontrollably, doubled up on the toilet seat, laughing like a madman – and in fact I am mad at this moment, I have stepped into the realm of madness, because I have broken a taboo.

A few minutes later, when my father has stamped his way back downstairs, my stomach rebels and pumps its multicoloured contents into the disinfected sink. Time itself seems to lurch inside me as I retch my mother's mixed grill out of my system and into that of the plumbing, which gurgles noisily as if in complaint. And through it all I am still shuddering with insane laughter.

I was still shuddering with insane laughter when Agnew returned. He looked disturbed, but intrigued to find me as I was, writhing in the chair helplessly.

'Are you all right?'

His concerned frown and solicitous hands – one on my shoulder, the other open and offering itself to be grasped, the fingers like such fat, pink sausages – made me worse. The spasm of laughter became all the more acute, and I could feel the sweat breaking out on my forehead and my face burning as I tried to contain it. Obviously he thought I was hysterical, or just mad, or both, but when I tried to suppress the laughter by looking away from him, I caught sight of the po-faced secretary, and that set me off again. He nodded to her and said something, and in a moment she was there with a glass of water. I took it and tried to drink it. I spluttered. I choked, I coughed. But, slowly, I was recovering, and Mr Agnew, experienced as he was in the many and diverse manifestations of grief, assured me that my reaction was very common, very common indeed, and that I was still in a state of shock, but that this would pass, it was a stage in my coming to terms with my loss.

Eventually I regained my composure, brushed the solicitous hand from my shoulder and said:

'Where's the body?'

Agnew led me along a short corridor from which several doors led off. He opened one of these and ushered me into a room that wasn't a room. It wasn't an ante-room either, because the coffin was there. I could see it out of the corner of my eye, along one wall, on a purpose-built shelf of some kind. I didn't look, but waited until he'd shut me in there with the corpse. He took a while to go. He hung around at the door, holding it open. I felt like telling him to fuck off and leave me alone with my father's corpse. Instead, I looked at him. That was enough to send him scuttling along the corridor, like a spider running away from some dangerous victim caught in its web.

There were subdued lights, tastefully concealed behind louvred panels, and from somewhere came the steady hiss of an air-conditioner. I half expected to hear some suitably morose Muzak to come wafting from concealed speakers, but no – this was Murkirk, not California. There was one upright chair, against the wall opposite the coffin. I moved it to the side of the coffin, but before I sat down, I looked.

The emaciation of the old man's head could not be disguised by its presentation, which involved a collar of fluted pink satin. The patina of powder and tint made it seem, if anything, less lifelike than the face of a corpse, slightly mask-like. The sharp ridges of the cheekbone and jaw were clearly visible, and his mouth, no doubt vivified by Agnew's hand, still looked like a rip in a piece of coarse canvas that had been sewn up hastily. The eyes, too, looked stitched shut.

The old man looked nothing like my father, though no doubt he had been someone's father. No doubt he had worked hard like my father, if not in the pits or the steelworks then in a factory or a brickworks. Or maybe not – who could tell?

I had a mind to complain about being shown the wrong cadaver, but, after all, I hadn't really come to see my father. I had come to see death and here was a good example of death. The fact that I didn't know the deceased hardly seemed to matter. At the same time, it was as if my father was mocking me. Hadn't he told me, the very night I'd thumped him, on the way back from the Dryburn Working Men's Club, that when he died I should come to see his dead body, because everyone had to see a dead body some time, because it was part of growing up? And now he'd dodged out of it, got someone else to stand in for him, reneged on our arrangement.

I sat there for a long time, paying scant attention to the corpse, but remembering that night in the Working Men's Club in Dryburn.

He's still mad at me for hitting him, although I've apologized, and he's feeling the need to get back at me. A pal of his, Aleck, has sat down with us, and when Aleck asks me what I'm studying, my father gets stuck in:

'Nietzsche by Christ. Slave for thirty year doon the flamin sufferin pit tae send him to the Uni and this is how he thanks me: Nietzsche!'

'What's wrong with Nietzsche, Dad?'

'He wants tae know what's wrong wi it! You tell him, Aleck – knock some sense intae him, will ye?'

Aleck shrugs and smiles, exposing the gaps in his teeth. He is an emaciated, unshaven, ferret-like man and his baggy brown raincoat makes him seem all the more skeletal as he moves around inside it restlessly, his beady, close-set eyes darting from his almost empty glass to the bar and back again.

'Eh . . . Ah wouldnae know about that. Only book Ah ever read was Wells what's-his-name.'

'H.G. Wells – great writer. *The War Of The Worlds*. *Invisible Man*. You tell him, Aleck.'

'Naw, eh . . . Wells Fargo, that's the boy.'

'Aye, Wells Fargo! He'd be better off readin that than what they're gien him up at the Uni! Nietzsche by Christ! A flamin sufferin Nazi.'

'No he wasn't, Dad! His philosophy was distorted by the Nazis! They *used* him!'

But I can hear the plea in my own voice, a shrill note that sounds like my mother.

My father flicks his ash with a disparaging gesture, brushing a smaller, weaker man aside.

'Oh? Is that so? The master race, eh? The Nazis used that – eh, Aleck?'

'Naw, Ah've definitely no read that wan. Ah dinnae go in for science fiction. Gimme a guid western any day.'

'Science fiction! Ye're right there, Aleck! The master race, by Christ – science fiction right enough!'

'But Dad, you've got to keep in mind the context—'

'Context! D'ye hear him, Aleck! D'ye hear what he's tryin tae tell me now, his faither, a trade union activist for twenty year in the pits! Context! Ah'll context ye, ya sod ye!'

Aleck smiles uncomfortably and says:

'Mine's identical. Cannae unnerstand a word he says since he went tae the college. Naw, Wells Fargo, that's what Ah enjoy.'

'Hear that? Here a man who's only read Wells Fargo, an you're tellin him tae think aboot the context! What d'ye mean, *context*?'

I take a long drink of my pint. I want to conceal my hesitation, or better still drop the subject, but my father won't let me off the hook:

'Eh?'

'I mean . . . the rest of his philosophy, Dad. In *Beyond Good and Evil*, his critique of Christianity—'

'Oh? There's anither context as well as that wan. It's cried History! It's cried Belsen! That right, Aleck?'

'Aw aye! History! Terrible stuff!' says Aleck, shaking his head from side to side vehemently and grimacing, as if history is a food he can't stand to eat and is scunnered by the very mention of. His eyes dart from father to son and back again, as if he's trying to work out what this argument really is about.

'I do know that, Dad, but Nietzsche thought—'

'Oh, ye do, do you? Would ye listen tae it, Aleck? Thinks he kens it aw, no let his auld faither tell him onythin!'

'Aye, mine's identical.'

'Hasnae even read Marx – wid ye credit that? Calls hissel educatit! Hasnae even read *The Ragged Trousered Fellae* an he talks tae his auld faither aboot Nietzsche. You've read *The Ragged Trousered Fellae*, eh Aleck?'

Aleck looks doubtful and moves around restlessly in his seat.

'Well, Ah might've read it a long time ago—'

'See? Aleck's read Robert Tressell an he's juist a panel-beater!'

'I've read it as well, Dad!'

'Oh, ye have, have ye? Mawn then – tell us what it's aboot.'

I open my mouth to begin, then shut it again and shake my head in exasperation, but my father persists:

'Mawn! Tell Aleck here what it's aboot, cause if ye cannae – what guid's yer flamin sufferin education, eh?'

'It's about this group of housepainters—'

'Naw it's no! It's aboot the oppression o the workin man by the rulin bloody classes – that right Aleck?'

Aleck, bewildered, agrees hastily.

'Calls hissel educatit! Doesnae even ken what *The Ragged Trousered Fellae*'s aboot! Needs an auld ex-miner like me tae explain it tae him!'

Aleck smiles uneasily and chips in:

'Eh . . . Ah couldnae say for sure Ah've read that wan masel. A good story, is it?'

'A *great book*. Shows the working man how tae fight back.'

I chip in:

'The only thing wrong with it's the ending.'

My father's eyes widen in outrage.

'Oh? Is that so? And what, for the benefit of us ornary workin men whae havnae read Nietzsche, is wrang wi the endin? *Eh*?'

I can hear the dangerous rise in his voice and I know I shouldn't pursue it, but there's no going back:

'He kills himself. It doesn't offer hope.'

'Ah like a happy endin masel,' suggests Aleck, tentatively.

'He kills hissel cause that's what happened! Robert Tressell committed suicide!'

'He died of tuberculosis, Dad.'

He waves this aside with a hand.

'Anywye, that's no the point, eh no, Aleck?'

Aleck shrugs and smiles, then, seeing that both me and my father are looking to him to settle the dispute, thinks better of his smile and starts nodding, then shaking his head furiously.

My father looks at me with exaggerated outrage.

'You'd bloody kill yersel if you'd had his life, ya swine ye!'

'Whose life, Dad? Tressell's or Frank Owen's?'

'Same thing, eh, Aleck?'

Aleck looks from my father to me and back again. He's clearly getting fed up with the argument.

'It's *not* the same thing, Dad! There's a difference between fiction and autobiography! Or there should be, but with *The*

Ragged Trousered Philanthropists, maybe there isn't, maybe that's what's wrong with it, maybe that's why it doesn't offer hope!'

But I know that I'm faltering, that I'm sounding muddled and strident, like a wee boy on the verge of a tantrum.

My father waves my words aside, laughing scornfully, then settles back in his chair and beams at Aleck, basking in his victory. It's as if all he has to do is get me arguing, get me riled and anxious to prove my point, then that proves that he's won.

'Would ye listen tae him, Aleck! That's how they're learnin him tae talk up at the Uni! Comes back here an tells us he's read Nietzsche, a flamin sufferin German fascist—'

'Aw leave him alane, he's just a boy. Mine's the same. They'll grow oot o it.'

Aleck leans over the table to me and consoles:

'Never mind him, son. You stick in at yer studies, eh? Here's tae ye, son!'

Aleck raises his glass and drains what's left in it.

'I'll get the drinks,' I say, as decisively as I can. I want to escape to the bar, but I'm not sure about whether the money in my pocket will cover the round.

My dad senses this and seizes on it:

'Oh ye will, will ye? Make mine a double. Aleck here'll have the same.'

'A wee nip'll dae me fine, son.'

'Naw it willnae. We'll have two doubles, and two half pints!'

I tug a handful of coins from my pocket and start to count them out on the table. It's obviously not enough. My father beams with satisfaction as he flourishes a ten-pound note.

'There ye are, ya fascist parasite! That's yer parental contribution! Keep the change! See that Aleck? He takes his poor auld faither's hard-earned money tae buy hissel books on reactionary German philosophy, then Ah have tae buy him his drinks! It's criminal, is it no?'

'Aye, mine's identical.'

I hear my father mention the Hitler Youth as I leave the table and suddenly everything seems comic, but with some of the tragic inevitability I remember from Aesthetics 1, in Aristotle's *Poetics*. Here I am, home, where I should belong, but don't feel that I do. Not any more. I look around the bar at the faces, all the faces of the men and the women here. Even if I want to be one of them – will they still have me?

A local band has set up their equipment on a small stage in a corner, and as I walk to the bar they start playing – there's no escaping it – 'The Green Green Grass of Home'.

But it's later, walking up the road from the club, that the subject comes up. I ask him what he thinks happens after death. Nothing, he says, but there's apprehension in his eyes. Then he tells me that by the time he was my age he'd seen plenty dead bodies, that it was part of growing up, but that I didn't have to look so down in the mouth about it – I'd see his soon enough.

So he knew he was going to die soon.

The knock at the door brought me back to the present. I hurried out. Agnew was still looking concerned about me. And there was something else in his look, as he showed me out to the front door, a kind of professional interest, as if I was an interesting example of something he'd heard of but not actually seen before, a rare species of mourner.

'All right?'

'It wasn't him.'

He smiled a sad smile, a smile laden with understanding and

condolence, a smile he had developed for the purpose, a smile that helped to explain the inexplicable:

'I know how you feel, many people feel the same when they lose someone they dearly love.'

Before closing the door behind me I looked over at the secretary and bleated at her again. She looked utterly terrified.

There was almost an hour to kill until there would be a bus to Dryburn – the godforsaken little village where my parents lived. It wasn't even home. They had moved there when my father's pit had been closed and he'd had to retrain as an engineer.

I meandered the streets of Murkirk with a restlessness I could barely contain. I passed Lemetti's Cafe, still the same glass door with the sign advertising coke, and the brass handle, where I'd spent so much time sitting around with schoolfriends after school and on Saturday afternoons.

I found myself outside the churchyard and I went in. It was a place I hadn't set foot in since schooldays, when I'd sometimes come here with Annie, my girlfriend at that time, for want of anywhere else to go. It seemed poorer now, shrunken and drab. Of course, we'd come here at night, when the darkness could be our accomplice. It had seemed a different place then, with darkness and a moon and the town clock gonging on the hour ... But I couldn't quite remember it in detail, couldn't remember how we'd talked to each other, couldn't quite see Annie's face in my mind. I was stuck in the present, in this crude, sweltering summer's afternoon. The graveyard seemed offensively public, giving so little privacy from the town around it that I found it hard to believe that we'd thought of it as *our* place. Now it looked like what it was for: a place where you dump the dead, with haste, then hurry away.

The older graves looked like badly made beds with lumpen blankets and awry headboards, as if the dead had bad dreams and were troubled by restless nights. Why did I see it like that, this ordinary little bit of ground? Why was I seeing everything like that today, as if everything had taken on a life of its own? My father had died, that must be it, and everything else was too alive. I felt something stirring inside me – a feeling to do with death maybe, or maybe it was to do with life. Either way, there was more disgust in it than loss. Maybe it was Sartre's *nausée*? Maybe I was going to throw up?

I wandered into the arched vestibule area of the church. The statues of the king and queen were still lying there, hands clasped on their chests, in their separate beds of stone. Though I'd often come in here with Annie, and we'd canoodled behind these outstretched, eroded figures, I'd paid no attention to them at the time. Now the figures had a surreal quality, as if the stone had become a thick fluid, a kind of dead grey jelly. Even the solid stone walls of the church, as I looked at them, seemed to clench and move apart like blackened knuckles, and the flagstones under my feet were like flesh. It seemed to me I could see the pores of the stone opening and closing. I walked over them to read an inscription above the statues and my foot disturbed a used condom among a heap of litter and leaves. That brought the pregnancy back and the image of a ghostly foetus I had seen in a colour supplement.

Go away, little ghost, don't haunt me.

Before the funeral everyone gathered at my sister Angela's house. My mother, buttoned up in her coat, a dark headscarf round her hair, sat on the edge of her chair and smoked her cigarette nervously. It was her usual way. There was nothing in her eyes or her voice to give away how she was feeling. My older brother Jim, dressed in a blue pin-striped suit that dated from before his marriage, from a dark time in his past when he had run a bingo hall in Doncaster, looked more careworn than the last time I'd seen him. Of course, he'd had to drive up from Norfolk, so maybe he was still tired from the journey. His blonde wife Rita, who'd always struck me as a happy person with a raunchy sense of humour, looked strangely subdued and uncomfortable in the grey dress she was wearing. Maybe it wasn't just the dress – we were all a bit uncomfortable. My other sister Carol, heavily pregnant, was feeling breathless and exhausted. Max, her boyfriend, usually such an easy-going guy – his hippy wedding to his ex-wife had been featured in the *Daily Mail* with a photograph and the caption: WOULD YOU LET YOUR DAUGHTER MARRY THIS MAN? – even he seemed on edge. And then there was me, with the black tie borrowed from one of my mum's neighbours and the suit jacket and corduroy jeans that didn't quite match for colour. I felt uneasy as well. Maybe we all felt a bit shabby in the room, which Angela had gone to great pains to decorate and furnish in a way that suggested both luxury and restraint. Angela didn't seem herself either – less business-like, less brisk. There were dark marks under her eyes – maybe she was just exhausted.

Of course, somebody was missing.

Only Arnold, Angela's husband, seemed perfectly at home in his role as host, serving out the drinks. When he'd done that, he stood in the bay-window and practised his golf swing as usual. He did it without thinking, it didn't matter where he was or who was in the room with him. It was like breathing.

He started talking about the death. He was talking to me, maybe just because I was nearest, but soon the others were listening as well. Apparently he'd been with him at the moment he'd died – when Angela had gone out of the room.

'I wouldn't have missed that experience for anything in the

world. I was talking to him, telling him what was in the paper, you know ... Ah, it's kind of problematic to communicate with someone who can't verbalize a response, especially a man like your father, a man who needed to talk. But, ah, he just looked at me and suddenly I knew he was going. It was, ah ... like he was *letting* go, then he looked at me and he said "Jesus Christ", and that was it. He went. He just went.'

'He went,' I repeated, under my breath. 'He went. He just went.'

My sister Carol was sitting beside me on the sofa, and she gave me a puzzled look.

I was finding it hard to keep down the laughter. What was this laughter inside me? This desperate, uncontrollable thing inside me that could only come out as laughter? Was it the divine laughter of Zarathustra, the cruel and remorseless laughter of the free spirit? Maybe not – anyway, I couldn't let it out, not here, not now. It would seem like I was being deliberately perverse.

My mother was taking in Arnold's words as if a great mystery was about to be revealed.

'Oh, would ye credit that!' she said.

My brother-in-law went on, glancing at me as he said:

'Strange last words for someone like your father, an old communist of his ah ... calibre, don't you think?'

I didn't really want to think about it at that moment, but like my father, my brother-in-law had the knack of coming out with things no one wanted to think about, the unwelcome truth – or, if that wasn't available, a provocative lie.

I didn't answer. I was looking at Carol, at the swelling under her dress. She was eight months pregnant. Birth was the mystery to me, the true horror, not death.

Angela countered her husband briskly:

'Oh for heaven's sake, Arnold, you're not seriously suggesting that Dad saw the light at the last minute! How ridiculous.'

'I'm not suggesting anything of the kind, all I'm saying is that you wouldn't expect a man of his political ah . . . disposition to ah . . . invoke the name of Christ with his last breath, that's all I'm saying.'

My mother, anxious to find some mystery here, blew her nose and, looking at the floor with wide, portentous eyes, ventured:

'Ye never know, Angela. He was a lapsed Catholic, remember.'

Angela closed her eyes with forbearance, then said in a measured voice:

'How could I forget? I was there when he threw the priest out of the house!'

My older brother Jim shifted around in his seat uncomfortably and said:

'You know Dad – he was probably swearing.'

Angela added:

'He was probably so sick of looking at you, Arnold, that he gave up the ghost!'

Arnold adjusted his grip on the four-iron and chipped an imaginary golf ball at her in reply.

My mother closed her eyes and said, as if pained:

'Oh, what a thing to say, Angela!'

But wasn't her reaction to Angela just like her reaction to my father? She felt more comfortable with Arnold's way of talking, because although she couldn't really understand it, he made everything sound like it had come out of a book.

At that moment I saw Carol's stomach move and she gasped. Everyone stopped talking. Max asked her:

'Was that the baby moving?'

Carol nodded and said it had been moving around a lot.

There followed a conversation about the position of the baby – apparently it wasn't in the right position. Everyone was eager to think of the birth rather than the death. Except me. I sat there staring at Carol's bulge with stupefied dread. No. Not for me. Not yet.

Carol noticed me looking at her and asked if I wanted to feel the baby kick. Then she took my hand and placed it on her stomach. After a moment, the baby kicked and I recoiled in horror, as if the baby had given me an electric shock. There was general laughter about this, then Jim said:

'Couldn't 've hurt that much!'

Rita laughed too loudly. Angela gave her a dirty look. Then she gave me a severe, questioning look – she knew something was up. When I left the room she came out after me and confronted me in the kitchen, so I told her that Polly might be pregnant. I found myself smiling a little as I told her – after all, being the youngest I was the only one who hadn't had kids, and I suppose part of me wanted to beat my breast in a manly display of potency, but Angela's reaction scared the hell out of me. It was like I'd told her that somebody had died: she shut her eyes, sagged into a chair and put her hands to her brow.

'Oh my God. She'll have an abortion.'

'I don't know if Polly would.'

Angela looked up at me in utter disbelief.

'But she must!'

Then my mother came through and I retreated into the back garden.

My nephews were playing football. Although there were only three of them, they were taking it seriously and for some reason I really wanted to join in, but when I did I felt awkward, I couldn't give myself to the activity of controlling the ball at my feet. Maybe my nephews sensed this, because they became strangely quiet as they passed the ball to and fro.

The phone rang just as the hearse arrived at the front door and everyone started getting ready to go. Angela answered it, then told me calmly, but it was as if she was restraining a scream, that it was Polly.

I hadn't expected her to call – she'd told me she'd be busy all day hanging her show. I told her I had to go, that the hearse was there outside.

'I just thought you'd like to know. My period's come.'

'Has it? Oh. That's good.'

Angela, who happened to be walking past me at that moment, squeezed my arm and closed her eyelids with relief.

Then everyone was walking past me through the hall and out the front door.

'Tell everyone I'm sorry I couldn't be there.'

'Sure, Polly. Good luck with your show. Everybody understands.'

'Will you be coming back tonight?'

'I said I'd stay a couple of days at my mum's.'

'Oh.'

She sounded disappointed.

'I won't stay long. A couple of days. Listen, Polly, I'm sorry about the other night . . . Things'll be better when I get back.'

'Will they?'

'Yeah. Everything changes, eh?'

She agreed with that although she sounded puzzled by it. I was puzzled by it myself, but it sounded like the right sort of thing to say under the circumstances.

Everyone looked at me strangely as I ran out of the door punching the air, unable to hide my jubilation. I was off the hook, I wasn't going to be a father, not yet. I was still free. First I had to help bury my father – if it was my father there in that long wooden box in the hearse.

If it was him. That was all I could think about during the ceremony. If Agnew could show me the wrong body in his funeral parlour, maybe he could make the same mistake when it came to burying him. We were all standing there looking long-faced, watching the coffin on the conveyor belt with squeaky wheels as it slowly disappeared into the dark place beyond the curtain, where presumably the cremation happened, but maybe we were attending the funeral of the old man I'd seen in Agnew's. I thought about him again now, and as the image of that lifeless head came into my mind, the certainty that it had in fact been my father struck me forcibly, almost as if my father himself had struck me a blow. Of course it had been him, there had been no mix-up with corpses! Confronted with his corpse, I had failed to recognize him – maybe I hadn't wanted to – and now my father jeered at me in my head. As the speaker from the Humanist Society went on with his little speech, my father's rasping, derisive laughter coursed through me like a pungent antidote. Jesus Christ, he was haunting me, the old bastard was taking me over! I had to let it out, but as soon as it started to come to my lips I tried to stifle it, so that I began to shake all over and splutter. The others were looking at me and I made a coughing fit out of it. When I'd recovered I glanced along the row at the others and saw that Carol too was shuddering, her head in her hands. But she was actually crying. I envied her. She'd cried after she'd seen him in intensive care, wearing the oxygen mask. Why hadn't I felt like that? I was impatient for the ceremony to be over. My mind kept asking me the wrong questions. How much was the visiting humanist paid to deliver the secular oration? Did they burn the coffins with the bodies, or did Agnew instruct his men to whip the bodies out and save the coffins from the flames – wouldn't that make sense? What a waste of good wood a coffin was, when you thought about it . . . and all those wasted flowers! The smell of them pervaded the place, and the claustrophobia of my own thoughts and the oppressive heat made me itch to be out.

*

The house was strange. My mother had been busy cleaning it, eradicating every trace of my father. I sat, slumped in front of the television, vaguely irritated by my mother's busyness. Wasn't there something strange about it? The way she had collected together all his clothes, washed and ironed them, then folded and tied them into neat bundles . . . it was weird. His other possessions, his razor, his shaving mug and mirror, his spectacles, his tobacco tins, his cigarette-rolling machine, his haversack for work, with its sandwich tin and its flask, his shoes, his walking sticks – all these relics of my father had been assiduously gathered together, some thrown away and others packeted and labelled and put in the bag with the clothes – the black plastic bag I was to take to the rest-home in Murkirk before I took the train back to Edinburgh.

My mother made me a cup of tea before I went. I looked around the room. It seemed different, tidier and more arid without my father, without the mess of newspapers and ash-trays and cups and plates he created. Still I could feel the back of my head settling into the dent in the armchair where his head had rested, despite the clean antimacassar she'd placed there.

'What did he look like, son?'

'How d'you mean, Mum?'

'Angela said his head went a funny colour all down one side just after he died.'

'It wasn't a funny colour when I saw him.'

'Did he look peaceful?'

'He just looked dead, Mum.'

She looked hurt and disappointed by that. I didn't want to get annoyed with her, but she was annoying me. The way she'd cleaned the house so briskly, obliterating all trace of my father. This business of having to take the bag of his things to a rest-home – as if the old folks waiting to die in there would appreciate a gift of a dead man's things. And what about me, what about my feelings? Didn't it occur to her that I might not enjoy taking this black bag of death to a rest home? And her curiosity about how he'd looked, as if she half regretted not having gone to look at the body herself. Now she wanted to know the details of its physical condition. It was her eagerness to find out about this that bothered me most and I wished I hadn't told her that I'd gone to Agnew's. Maybe, like me, it hadn't come home to her yet that he was really dead. Maybe like me, she had yet to feel the loss.

I kissed my mother and asked her if she'd be all right on her own. She told me she would, that she had her work to go back to in the morning and that she could always phone up Angela if she needed to talk to somebody. I picked up my bag and slung it over my shoulder, then said goodbye and heaved the other bag on to my other shoulder. It was heavy.

My mother stood at the window until I reached the gate, then she waved. I held up my one free hand in reply. Then I watched her adjust her glasses, look along the street first one way then the other way, before turning away from the window and going to meet herself. It was the first time she'd been left alone since he'd died. It was probably the first time she'd been alone for a long time – maybe she'd never really been alone? I wondered what she'd do, what she'd think about in that empty house on her own.

When the bus moved off, the bag sagged forward and let out some air. It made a noise that was eerily human, like a sigh of resignation. Every time the bus turned a corner the bag leaned towards me a little. It kept shifting its position in the seat, as if it wasn't comfortable. When the bus stopped at a bus stop and people came on, I noticed them glancing at the bag. Maybe they wondered what was in it. I knew. I knew what was in it all right, and for the first time I had a sense of my father's sudden absence, and the huge emptiness he left behind him. It was inside me, that sudden absence, that huge emptiness, and I wondered if it would ever shrink or be filled.

As the bus moved off, the bag lurched forward in the seat and I had to catch it to stop it falling. For the rest of the journey I kept my hand on it, holding it steady on the seat beside me. It made a strange passenger.

The Fight

He was going to see a fight.

'Shut your ears,' said his father.

He didn't think he really meant him to put his hands over his ears, he meant don't listen to the language. He tried not to, but the more you tried not to hear the language, the more you couldn't help hearing it. Even if you covered your ears with your hands, like he'd done once when he'd heard his mother screaming and shouting about something his father had done in Gorebridge, even with your ears covered you still heard things – your breathing in and breathing out, your heart beating, your throat swallowing. It was incredible if you did it when you were eating crisps. It sounded like an avalanche.

An avalanche was something he liked to think about. He liked the idea of it starting with one wee stone rolling down a mountain, then it bumped into another wee stone and it started rolling down the mountain as well. The two wee stones rolled faster and faster, then bumped into another two stones a bit bigger, then they started rolling down the mountain as well. So four stones bumped into another four, making eight, then they bumped into another eight, then the sixteen became thirty-two, then sixty-four, then a hundred-and-something and then it was an avalanche.

Even if he did cover his ears, he knew he'd still hear the voices coming nearer in the night, the men's voices cursing and swearing and singing, only they'd sound like they were inside him, like the cursing and swearing and singing was coming from him and not from not-him.

He tried shutting his eyes instead, but that just made the voices sound nearer, and the cheesy smell of the brewery and the rain smelled stronger, and the muddy path felt squelchier. And shutting your eyes didn't stop you seeing things, just the same as covering your ears didn't stop you hearing things. Even when you were sleeping, you kept seeing things. The only way to stop hearing things and seeing things and smelling things was to be dead. He tried to imagine what it would be like to be dead, to be not-him. It might be like being a stone.

He bent down and picked up one that was lying on the path. It looked dark but shiny in his hand. He put it in his pocket and felt it. It felt wet and slippy and jaggy. It had a sharp corner and a secret rounded part and a flat bit. It was just a thing, but maybe things were really alive inside of themselves, maybe the stone in his pocket was really glad that he'd picked it up. Maybe it had been lying on the path for ages just hoping to be picked up by somebody and taken somewhere else. When he clenched it tight in his hand it cut into his palm and hurt him. How could a thing that could hurt you like that be dead? Maybe being dead wouldn't be like being a stone after all, maybe you just floated around in space not hearing or seeing or smelling or touching or tasting anything, because how could you without ears and eyes and a nose and hands and a mouth? But maybe you just floated around above the clouds having memories and dreams. Maybe you could still have memories and dreams even without a brain to have them in, but he couldn't really imagine that – but maybe the only reason he couldn't really imagine it was that he was an atheist.

The sky looked orange, not like the sky where he lived. There were no fields in Edinburgh, just houses and streets and the orange light from the streetlamps. They were walking over a muddy stretch of wasteground where there were no street-lights. Somebody, one of his dad's friends, knew the way, and everybody was walking behind him in single file.

He wished he'd stayed at home with his mum and his sisters. At this very moment he'd be sitting on the floor beside his mum's chair in front of the fire, watching Harry Worth doing the thing on the corner of the shop window, raising one arm and one leg and making it look like both. Before he'd left, he'd eaten a bowl of broth with barley and golden bubbles in it. He'd supped up the golden bubbles and left the barley at the bottom of the bowl. Now he felt hungry and wished he'd eaten the barley as well. She'd made him wear his Burberry. He hadn't wanted to wear it, but now he was glad of it.

The voices were coming nearer all the time. There were too many of them. It was a song. They weren't singing it though, they were shouting it:

'*Hullo, hullo*, we are the Billy boys! *Hullo, hullo—*'

So that was who they were. They were Protestants and they went to an Orange lodge every Tuesday night. His big brother had gone along to join the Orange band to learn to play the drums, then his dad had given him hell about it, so his big brother hadn't been able to go back. But then his big brother had saved up for a drum kit and had joined a band called The Trailblazers and had run away from home to start a new life in Doncaster.

His big sisters had told him about a Catholic school they'd gone to before his dad had an argument with the priest and told him never to darken his doorway with his mendacious propaganda again, and that was why he'd got sent to a Protestant school and his big sisters had got moved from the Catholic school to the Protestant school.

It was OK being an atheist except his dad always gave him a note to stop him going to the church at the end of term. He'd asked his dad why he couldn't go and and he'd said it was because he was an atheist who didn't believe in God and he only sent him to the Protestant school because it wasn't as bad as the Catholic school, because there wasn't a school for atheists.

So when all the other kids went to the church he had to go to the sick-room. That was OK except everybody took the piss out of him and called him a heathen. Sometimes just being in the sick-room made him feel sick. Once he'd really been sick into the sink and the nurse had put her hand on his forehead while he was being sick. He could still remember how cool her hand had felt on his forehead and how he'd wondered why she was being so kind. Maybe she didn't believe in God either, maybe atheists helped each other to be sick and had cool hands to hold each other's hot foreheads.

There was a burn in the middle of the wasteground. He could hear it trickling in the dark but it was too dark to see. Now that it was happening he knew it was the way it had to happen: they reached the burn at the same time as the shouting men. Maybe there was going to be a fight on the way to see the fight. He held the stone tighter in his pocket, so that he could feel its hardness cutting into his fingers and his palm. It was alive, and if there was a fight he'd send the stone flying through the air at one of the other men. The stone would enjoy that, because if you were a stone probably the only excitement you got was when somebody threw you. He could just imagine how it would feel, to be stuck in one place for years and years, then somebody notices you and picks you up and sends you flying through the air or rolling down a mountain.

Across the burn somebody had put planks of wood for a bridge. His father's friends were silent as they crossed the plank bridge and came face to face with the other men. It was like they were going to a funeral. Then he heard his father say:

'Awright boys? Mind the wean, eh?'

Then he knew everything was under control. The men who were shouting made a great thing about standing aside and letting him past. One of them smiled at him before drinking out of a bottle. One or two hands patted his head. It felt good to see all these men standing aside for him, but it didn't feel so good to be called the wean. He was glad he was with the men who were silent, not the shouting men. He knew they were strong, as strong as any men could be, strong inside as well as with their hands, because they were miners. If a fight did start, they would win. And even if they didn't win, they would fight as well as they could, they would stand by each other, and so even if they lost the losing would be almost like winning.

Now that he was passing the other men he could see they were younger. One or two of them had Elvis haircuts and white shirts and thin black ties, like his big brother. Some of them weren't really men yet, they were still just big boys.

He took his father's hand and they walked on across the wet, dark wasteground. He was glad when they came to a lane that led up to a street and there were streetlights again and pavements.

'Da, are we nearly there?'

'Aye, we're here.'

They crossed the road to a big building that looked like a warehouse. The light from the doorway crossed the street and climbed up the wall on the other side.

It was good to see the bright light on the boxing ring and to drink his Bovril and eat his hot pie. The men around him kept smiling and winking at him and pretending to punch him on the jaw. One of them nodded at him and said to his father:

'Get him in the ring, get the gloves on him.'

His father gave him the programme and pointed out which boxers were from the Rosewell gym. He pointed to a name and said:

'Les. He's our new boy.'

He knew Les. Les had done a paper round before he'd left school to go down the pit and sometimes he'd tagged along helping him to deliver the papers.

He could smell beer, wet coats, Brylcreem and a vinegary smell that made his stomach shrink.

The first fight was fast. The two boxers didn't dance around like he'd seen boxers doing on TV. They just wheeled round in the middle of the ring and battered each other. At the same time they kept hanging on to each other as if they wanted to have a cuddle.

He looked round at all the men watching the fight. That was worse to see than the fight. They were all shouting and snarling and punching the air with their fists. Then he looked along the row at the miners. They were laughing. And now that he looked at the boxers, they were throwing punches at each other so fast that it did look quite funny, like a cartoon. His father had a big grin on his face and said to the man next to him:

'Need tae get that pair on the march!'

Sometimes all the miners got together and went on a march. It meant they all walked along the road together from one town to another town. Sometimes they had these big banners with words written on then in golden letters. They all sang songs as they walked along the road together, but it was really another kind of fight. He had heard about a march some miners had gone on to see a prime minister, who lived in a house in London with a policeman out-side the door. He had seen the policeman once on the news. He felt sorry for him. Imagine having to stand outside somebody's door all day not doing anything. He imagined the policeman standing there all day wishing it was lousing time so that he could get home and get his tea. Then he would sit down by the fire with a big plate of steak pie and chips on his knee and maybe he'd see himself standing outside the door on the news and he'd say to his wife and his kids, 'Look, that's me.'

The last march his father had gone on had been to Hawick and he'd brought him back a pair of boxing gloves. He'd woken up in the morning and they'd been hanging on the headboard of the bed. He'd put them on right away, jumped out of bed and started boxing his reflection in the mirror.

It was Les's first fight. When he climbed between the ropes and stood in the glaring light he looked dazed, like an animal kept in a cage underground for a long time, then let out in the sunshine. He had curly black hair and the kind of eyebrows that slanted up in the middle. He looked around at the crowd and blinked his eyes. Then the trainer put his gumshield in his mouth and started shouting into his ear. Les kept nodding at what the trainer was shouting in his ear and sniffing his gloves and blinking his eyes.

The bell rang and Les went out to meet the other boxer, who was from Gorebridge. The boxer from Gorebridge had a ginger crew-cut and as soon as the bell rang and the fight started, he punched Les on the head and knocked him down. All the miners were shouting to Les to get up. Les lay on the floor of the ring while the referee counted. He started to get up, but it was too late. He was out. The fight was finished.

As Les climbed out of the ring, the miners shouted to him:

'Never mind, son!'

'Ye'll be awright next time!'

One or two of them stood up and went over to Les to pat his shoulder. Les kept shaking his head and blinking his eyes and asking what had happened.

There were other bouts and some of them had boxers who were from the Rosewell gym. The miners were up on their feet, shouting and punching the air like the other men. All except for two men who were wearing black suits and bow-ties. They were the judges and nobody knew where they came from. He wondered if they always wore the black suits and the bow-ties, even when they were sitting in their living rooms having their teas.

He was put in the snug and his father got him some lemonade and a packet of crisps and left him there. It was good to be on his own at last, just to see the shadows of the men on the frosted glass without having to see them and listen to them. The walls of the snug didn't go up to the ceiling and he could hear all their voices, talking and laughing. When he had finished his crisps and lemonade, he started pretending to be a boxer, to be Les, to be knocked out with the first punch. He played at losing, like in the game of best deaths they sometimes played on the railway embankment. What happened was that one of you went up to the top, everybody else shot you, then you fell off your horse and rolled down to the bottom and died. Everybody got a shot of getting shot, then everybody voted to choose the best death. You couldn't choose your own death, of course, you had to vote for somebody else's. He liked being shot, he liked falling, then rolling down the embankment and lying completely still. When he'd played at cowboys and Indians, it had always been more fun to be an Indian, a bareback rider, wearing warpaint and feathers, firing arrows and spears and yelling wallawalla-wooska, shot from your horse to roll over and over in the dust and die – that was better than blowing a bugle and firing a gun.

He danced around, pretending to be in the ring and to be knocked out, to fall on the floor then start to get up, to be counted out, to lose. To be led out of the ring with your head hung down and everybody patting you on the back and telling you it was all right.

He had to stop when two other boys were brought into the snug. They'd been at the fight as well, but they were from Gorebridge. The older boy was wearing a Burberry exactly like his, except that it was dark blue rather than dark green. He had a freckly face, and his black hair hung over one eye at the front. He had a big nose with a bump in the middle of it. The younger boy had sticking-out ears and hunched shoulders, like he was trying to hide his neck, and he was waiting to see what the older boy would do.

'Where d'you come frae?' said the older boy.

'Rosewell.'

The older boy looked at the younger one and sneered. The younger boy grinned.

'Ye a Proddy?'

He shook his head.

'So ye're a Pape, eh?'

He shook his head again.

'What are ye then, a fuckin Mormon?'

He thought about pretending he was a Mormon, but he knew this boy wouldn't let him away with it, he'd find out he was lying.

'Ah'm a atheist.'

'A what?'

'A atheist. I don't believe in God.'

'Aw aye, a atheist, eh? But are ye a Prodestant atheist or a Catholic atheist? Eh?'

The boy started poking him in the chest with his finger and repeating:

'Eh? Eh?'

He could feel his heart hammering, like somebody running, and the dizzy feeling in his head. There was a heavy feeling in his belly like he was going to be sick, then he smelled the vinegary smell and knew what it reminded him of. It reminded him of other fights he'd had, of how he'd felt before the fight, scared and excited.

The older boy was pushing him against the wall. Already something had come loose inside him, he could feel it moving, growing. And everything had been leading up to this, this was what the whole night was really about. It was all right losing when you were playing at losing, but not when it was real. The boy pushed him harder against the wall and he could feel the thing inside moving faster, like stones rolling in his head. They held each other and wheeled round and fell, then the boy was on the floor and he was on top of him and his hard fists drummed against the boy's hard head as the stones and boulders rolled and bounced and collided out of control in his head, and his heart hammered faster and his fists drummed harder and the boy's bloodied face blurred with the tears because he couldn't stop, couldn't stop it because it wasn't him, it came from not-him, rolling and crashing through him like an avalanche.

The door of the snug opened and his father stood there shouting:

'What in hell's fire is going on in here?'

He stood up. The other boy stood up as well and started crying loudly, then the younger boy joined in.

He had been crying too, but now he stopped. He hung his head, afraid of what his father would do. Even although the other boy had started it, he knew that because he'd won, he'd get the blame.

The Face

He didn't want to see the face.

It was like a railway tunnel, except this tunnel sloped down the way, down through the dripping darkness, down into the deep, dark ground. He could see the dark shine of the rails and he could feel the ridges of the wooden sleepers through the soles of his gymshoes. It was very dark. He was glad his father was there with him.

It would be good to go back up to the daylight now, where the miners were sitting round a brazier, eating their pieces and drinking hot tea from big tins with wire handles. One of them had given him a piece and let him drink some tea from his tin and had pointed to different birds and told him their names, while the other miners talked about the pit and how it was closing. One of them had said he'd be quite happy never to see the face again.

He remembered the first time he'd heard about it: his father came in late from the pit and walked into the kitchen very slowly and sat down still with his coat on. Then he took off his bunnet and looked at it and put it on the kitchen table and talked to his mother in the quiet voice not like his usual voice. Like he couldn't say what he had to say, like when some of the words get swallowed. Because somebody had got killed at the face, John Ireland had got killed at the face, so he'd had to go to Rosewell to tell his wife. That was why he was late. Then his mother took a hanky from her apron pocket and sat down and started crying and his father put his hands on her shoulders and kissed her like it was Christmas except this was a different kind of kiss. Then his father looked up at him and nodded to him to tell him to go through to the other room, so he went through and watched TV and wondered how the face had killed John Ireland, the man who ran the boxing gym for boys, and how something terrible could make people need to kiss each other.

He could hear the water dripping from the roof of the tunnel and trickling down the walls and the scrape and crunch of his father's boots on the ground. They sounded too loud, but in the dark you had to hold on to sounds, like when you shut your eyes and pretended to be blind, hold on to them to stop yourself hearing what was behind them, where it was like the darkness was listening.

Every few steps he could see the wooden props against the walls, but they were nearly as dark as the walls. And he could just make out the shapes of the wooden sleepers and the rails, but he didn't like the darkness between the sleepers and between the props. If you looked at darkness like that too long you started seeing things in it: patterns, shapes, faces . . .

He listened to his father's voice. It sounded too loud, and crackly like a fire, but you could hold on to it. He was telling him about the bogies that used to run up and down on the rails in the old days, taking the coal up to the pit-head. It was good to hear his father's voice talking about the old days, but he didn't like the sound of the bogies. He asked what a bogie was and listened as his father told him it was sort of like a railway carriage on a goods train. He knew that anyway, but he wanted to hear his father telling him again, just in case.

There were other bogeys – bogeymen. He asked if there

were bogeymen down the pit. His father laughed and said that there weren't. But he knew different, he knew that it was dark enough down here for bogeymen, especially now the word had been said out loud.

Sometimes if you said a word over and over again it started to sound different. It started to mean something else, to mean what it sounded like it meant. Then, if you kept on saying it over and over again, it started to not mean anything, the word started to be a thing. And the thing didn't mean anything except what it was.

He tried it now, saying it under his breath over and over again . . . But before the word could lose its meaning, his father had stopped walking. He stopped too and turned, glad that they were going to go back up to the light, to the ordinary world.

'You go on.'

At first he wondered what his father meant, then he knew: he wanted him to keep on walking down into the dark. Alone. He pretended not to have heard and took a step towards the start of the tunnel, then he felt his father's hand on his shoulder and his heart pounding in his chest.

'Down ye go.'

He didn't move. He didn't say anything, hoping his father would lose his patience with him and change his mind.

'Are ye feart?'

'Naw, but . . .'

But what? He turned to the darkness. He could still see the rails and the props and the sleepers, but only just. He didn't want to see the face.

'Go on.'

He started walking down into the darkness. He had sometimes seen it in his dreams, after his father had come home late and spoken in the quiet voice to his mother about John

Ireland: at first there was just the dark, the pitch-black dark that was blacker than coal, because even coal wasn't always black, because sometimes it was blue or grey, and sometimes it had a dark shine to it, like the cover of the Bible, and sometimes the coal had seams – of fool's gold, or the thin, brittle, silvery seams of mica – but the darkness in the dream had no shine to it, no seams, it was pure black. Then you felt it there like a shadow in the dark, a shadow that went long and went wide, went thick like a wall and went thin like a thread, then the shadow had the shape of a man and the man had a face and the face was the face of John Ireland.

He stopped walking, turned around and looked back at his father. He called to him and asked if he'd gone far enough.

'Further.'

It was good to hear his father's voice behind him, but it didn't last long enough to hold on to. Why didn't his father walk down further too? Why did he have to walk down on his own? Sometimes his father liked him to walk in front of him along the street. 'Walk in front,' he'd say, 'where I can see you.' Like the time he'd taken him to the gym to see John Ireland and he'd seen John Ireland's face. It looked like a bulldog's, with a flattened nose and a crushed ear and big, bloodshot eyes. In the dream it looked worse. In the dream, somehow you forgot it was the face of an old boxer. John Ireland had given him a pair of boxing gloves. He'd tied them together and put them round his neck on the way home. And his father had told him to walk in front, where he could see him. But that wasn't the reason, not the real reason he wanted him to walk in front. It was because he wanted to dream about his son being a champion boxer. He hadn't gone back to the gym because his mother had put her foot down, but he still put the gloves on sometimes and pretended to be a champion boxer. Now there wasn't a gym because of what had happened at the face.

Maybe it wouldn't be like the face in his dream, but he still didn't want to see it. He stopped and turned around. He could still see the dark shape of his father against the light from the start of the tunnel. He shouted to him and waited.

'Go on.'

His father's voice faded to an echo.

He turned and walked further down into the dark, the pitch-black dark even blacker than coal, then he felt it there, a shadow in the dark . . . He stopped, turned and shouted to his father. He could still see the dim greyish light from the start of the tunnel, but now he couldn't see his father. He shouted out again. His own voice echoed and he heard the fear in it, then all there was was the listening darkness all around and the pounding of his heart. The shadow had the shape of a man and the man had a face . . .

As he turned to run away he was lifted in the air and his father's laughter filled his ear. He was laughing and saying he was proud, proud of him because he'd walked down on his own, proud because now he was a man.

He rubbed the bus window with his hand and looked out at the big black wheel of the pit. He watched it getting smaller as the bus pulled away, till it was out of sight.

'Da? Why are they gonnae shut the pit? Is there nae coal left in it?'

'There's plenty coal.'

'How then?'

'The government wants it shut.'

'Where'll ye go tae work then?'

'Mibbe in Bilston Glen.'

'Is that another pit?'

His father nodded. He waited a minute, then he asked:

'Da? Has it got a face as well?'

'Aye, it's got a face.'

'Is it like the face in your pit?'

His father shrugged.

'Much the same.'

'Da . . . Ah *saw* it.'

'What?'

'The face.'

His father shook his head and smiled at him, the way he did when he thought he was too young to understand something.

'Ah did see it!'

'Oh ye did, did ye? What did it look like then, eh?'

'It looked like the man who ran the gym.'

And he knew he'd said something very important when his father stopped smiling, turned pale, opened his mouth to say something but didn't say anything, then stared and stared at him – as if he couldn't see him at all, but only the face of the dead man.

Spirit, Tinder And Taboo

'Fancy some bubble gum?'

He shook his head. Derek Logan dug him in the arm with an elbow and, looking over his shoulder to make sure nobody was watching, passed him the card. He took it but didn't turn it over. The conductor was coming up the stairs. He held the card against his leg and waited. Derek nodded at it, made his eyes go cock-eyed and blew up his cheeks. Like somebody trying to blow up a balloon. One that wouldn't blow up.

'Take a dekko at that.'

A dekko. That was a daft-sounding word. He didn't like it. Since the thing had happened, some words sounded different, sounded like they meant more than before. Other words just sounded dafter. 'Dafter' sounded dafter. Every word still meant the same, but now it was like he was listening to them inside his head one at a time. Fancy. Some. Bubble. Gum.

Derek popped a square of it into his mouth, then made another face: he narrowed his eyes and tightened his lips and looked as evil as he could, but he was too freckly-cheeked and curly-haired and *glaiket* to look evil.

Glaiket. It was one of the words you said all the time but got told off for if you wrote. Words like scunner and smirr and girn and nyaff and grue and eedjit and dreich and wheesht. You knew what they all meant but you didn't write them because you got told off for it. Even if you wanted to write them you didn't know how to spell them, because they weren't in the dictionary, because they weren't real words.

He knew he could make a much better evil face than Derek, a really evil face. All he had to do was feel evil, because he was evil. The power that had come into him that night had felt so strong it had scared him. It was still there, coiled inside him like a whip. Now all he had to do was reach down and take it in his hand.

Suddenly he thought of a word he didn't know he knew. He said it out loud:

'Whippersnapper.'

'Eh?'

He looked at Derek, but didn't say anything else. Derek looked puzzled, then started whistling through the space between his big yellow front teeth and dug him with his elbow again. He took his rolled-up towel from under his arm calmly, moved it to under the other arm, then stabbed his elbow into Derek's arm as hard as he could. Derek squealed with pain. It felt good to really hurt his friend, even though he knew Derek would really hurt him back. They started having a serious battle of elbows and the card slipped off his leg just when the conductor came up.

It landed face-up. The conductor bent down and picked it up. The conductor looked at the photograph on the card for a long time, while the two of them sat tight, arms folded, and stared straight ahead. He glanced out of the corner of his eye at Derek. His cheeks had gone a deep red. He could feel the heat in his own face, but he tried to look grown up. After all, he was one of them now – he knew all about spirit, tinder and taboo.

The conductor wasn't saying anything. He was just standing there looking at them, as if they were really far away and he could hardly see them. Then he shook his head really slowly and said:

'Well, well, well . . .'

The conductor leaned down to them and held out the card. When he took it, the conductor said:

'Yer big sister, is it?'

The bus stopped and the conductor took their fares. Before he ran downstairs, he turned to grin at them and said:

'Tell her Ah'm loused at six!'

Loused. It was one of the words his dad used. It meant finished work for the day. It sounded like one of the words that weren't real words.

Derek giggled. He started giggling too, then stopped himself. He wasn't a kid any more. He had grown up that night, lying in bed thinking about Shiona Fraser and the women on the bubble-gum cards.

Sometimes they wore bikinis, sometimes see-through negligees, sometimes black lacy bras and knickers, suspenders and stockings. Usually they had high heels. There were even a few without bras, but they were rare. Collector's items. He'd swapped Derek three brand new prehistoric monsters and a golf ball for one of them.

The cards were better than the underwear pages in his mum's catalogue, because the women on the cards looked at you in a different way. It was what they did with their bodies, the positions they sat in or kneeled in or stood in, the way they leaned forward or leaned back, twisted and turned – but most of all it was the way they looked at you. Sometimes it was just the eyes that did it. They had this evil look in them. They were the ones he liked best.

It was incredible – and it all came with the bubble gum they bought in Jeannie's shop, next to the Scout hut. Last summer it had been ginger beer. They'd decided ginger beer was the thing to drink. They'd drunk it every day, so Jeannie had had to order crates and crates of the stuff to keep them going. This summer it was the bubble-gum cards they couldn't get enough of. They'd go in and buy twenty packets at a time. What you were supposed to do with all that bubble gum, he didn't know. Sometimes he wondered about it – maybe it was just ordinary bubble gum, but coming in a packet with a nearly nude woman made it almost taste different. It was pink, dusted with some sweet white powder and smelled like his wee sister when she got out the bath.

The only thing was, you had to keep the cards hidden. One night last week his mum had found some of them in his pocket when she'd ironed his jeans. She'd said something to him about it – his own mother! She'd asked him where he'd got them and said it was a damned disgrace. He wanted to shut his eyes and hide his face in his hands when he thought of his mum ironing his jeans and saying that.

The only other time he'd felt like that was when Miss Neilsen, his teacher in primary school, had heard him calling Derek a cunt. She hadn't said anything about it, and that had made him feel even worse. It was the look on her face that had made him feel so bad – as if he'd wounded her.

It was one of the words you weren't allowed to write *or* say. You had to hide it from the adults. But there was a memory in his mind of going into his mum and dad's bedroom one night when he was younger. And his dad had lifted him into the bed and laid him down between them, and he had listened to the both of them breathing on either side of him, and then they had started talking in a way that they didn't talk usually. And what was different about it was the nearness of the voices to each other, as if the voices were reaching out and touching each other in the darkness. And he'd lain there in the warm dark cave of the bed between them, listening to their voices for a long time, then he had heard his dad saying the word 'cunt' very softly, and it hadn't sounded like he was swearing at all.

He glanced at the card. She was sitting on a high stool with her legs crossed. She was pushing one of her shoulders out and bringing her hands up in front of her, as if the photographer had taken her by surprise. Her blonde, back-combed hair and her high, pencilled eyebrows made the surprise look sort of fixed. There must be a word for it.

Permanent. That was one of the words that meant more than before. A bit sinister. Sinister. That was another one.

Derek leaned into him as the bus turned the corner to look at the picture with him. He glanced at Derek looking at the woman on the card. He'd seen the same expression on his face before – he'd been looking at something he really wanted but knew he couldn't get: a rifle, in the window of a shop that sold fishing tackle and hunting gear.

'She's a brammer, eh?'

A brammer. He definitely wasn't going to say that one any more – it was childish. But what was she wearing? Now that he looked closely, he saw that she was wearing nothing. That was why Derek was making the faces. She was the first one either of them had seen who was completely nude. He shrugged and passed the card back. Derek grabbed it out of his hand and said:

'What a *brammer*, eh?'

'She's OK.'

Derek looked at him askance and held the card up to his face.

He shoved the hand with the card away.

Derek looked personally hurt, squeezed the card back into his jeans pocket, folded his arms and stared out of the bus window. That was it, he was going in the huff.

Sometimes the ones wearing bras were better than the ones that weren't anyway. Was it the underwear that was sexy or the actual body? Sometimes the nipples reminded him of the red rubber heads on the arrows of a toy bow-and-arrow set he'd got for his birthday when he was ten. If you licked the rubber head, when you fired the arrow it stuck to the door or the wall or the window. It was when you took the rubber head off the wooden shaft and turned it round that it looked like a nipple. At least, it looked like how he imagined a real nipple would look. Nipple. What a word that was. It sounded just like what it meant.

He still had the bow and arrows, and that night he'd got fed up sitting in his room looking at the cards of the women, so he'd pinned them all up on his bedroom wall and fired the arrows at them. It had felt like a strange thing to do. He'd gone on doing it until he'd heard his dad coming up the stairs, then he'd ripped all the cards down in a panic in case he came into the room. He'd got into his bed and started thinking about Shiona Fraser.

She lived round the corner, about half-way between his house and Derek's. She was the same age, but she looked older. She wore make-up and nail varnish to school. He'd heard stories that she'd actually done it with boys. He didn't know if they were true or not. In a way, he hoped they weren't. Once, sitting beside her in the class, his hand had brushed against her leg and he'd been amazed at how rough her tights had felt. She hadn't moved. She'd sat there completely still. Was that because she'd felt it or because she hadn't? Was she trying to think about the touch or trying to ignore it?

Another time, at the baths, Derek had pushed him into her. In the confusion of arms and legs as they fell under the water, his hand had landed on her breast. He'd expected it to feel hard, but it had been soft like a blancmange. This had come as a disappointment at the time, but that night in bed he'd remembered the softness again and it had excited him. Shiona

Fraser in her bathing suit had blurred with some of the women on the cards. The power had come into him, then his prick had reared up and spurted the hot sticky stuff called spunk.

It wasn't a word you were allowed to say or write *or* think, but although it sounded Scottish and it was dirty and it was a swear word, he'd been amazed to find it in the dictionary. It meant a lot of things. It meant spirit. It meant tinder. It meant *taboo*. He didn't know what *taboo* meant and hadn't bothered to look it up. It sounded African. Maybe it was the African word for it. The Scottish word for it sounded so dirty, you even felt guilty for thinking it.

He remembered Derek telling him, when they were still in primary school, that you got it in the middle of golf balls as well. He'd challenged him to prove it, and Derek had gone and got a golf ball and cut it open with a pen-knife. He'd peeled away the hard white plastic, then unwound the thin rubber bands inside until he'd got to a wee black rubber ball in the middle. When he'd stuck the pen-knife into it, some white liquid had spurted out. He remembered Derek wondering how the fuck they had got it inside golf balls.

He looked at his friend and laughed at him, at the memory. Derek went on looking out of the window, his arms folded, in the huff. He wouldn't be able to keep it up for long. Already he'd started blowing bubbles with his bubble gum. Soon he'd make one of them pop, then he'd giggle and start carrying on again. He wished he wouldn't. He wasn't in the mood for it. He wasn't in the mood for anything except the baths.

They had been coming to the baths two or three times a week during the summer holidays. McAllister, the attendant, usually just nodded to them as they paid their money. Today, when he passed the rubber wristbands through the hole in the window, he wouldn't let them go. He stood there on the other side of the glass, not smiling but looking pleased with himself. Sometimes he pretended to be a bit mad to make them laugh. He was a thin, clean-shaven man with very red skin, very white teeth and shiny, neatly cut black hair. Somehow he managed to make his navy blue track-suit and white tee-shirt look like a sailor's uniform. Maybe it was the silver whistle that did it. It hung round his neck on a length of scarlet elastic, almost like a medal.

He'd played this game before with the rubber wristbands.

Derek started trying to tug them from his hand, but McAllister wasn't letting go. He raised one of his liquorice-stick eyebrows and said:

'Well, boys. Have yous done it yet then?'

It was the way he looked at him as he said it, as if he knew. Maybe people could tell just by looking at you. Maybe it showed.

'Done what?'

McAllister ignored Derek and kept looking him in the eye. He curled his lips into a smile and said:

'Learnt to swim, boys, learnt to swim.'

McAllister let the wristbands go and they ran up the steps, through the glass door and alongside the pool. Derek was racing to a cubicle, anxious to get changed quick and be in the water first. He let him. It was good to see the pool completely still. It looked like a mirror lying flat on its back, reflecting the sky. It made him feel calm just looking at it. He didn't want to race. He wanted to do everything slowly, because everything felt a bit different. The smell of the chlorine, the reflections of the windows on the water, the way their voices seemed to stretch and bend and echo off the walls and the ceiling ... Maybe everything was the same as usual, but he was just noticing it more.

He heard Derek shouting and the splash when he jumped in.

He stood on the wooden seat to look over the door at him. McAllister passed by, whistling, a towel round his neck, and glanced in at him. That was something he sometimes did. Sometimes, after their swim, when they were getting dried, he came and stuck his head over the cubicle doors and told them to get a move on because other folk were waiting to use the cubicles. Or sometimes just to ask questions. What street they lived in. What school they went to. What their dads did.

When he came out of the cubicle, Derek was already climbing back out of the pool, complaining that the water was freezing. Derek shivered and made his teeth chatter more than he needed to. They hurried to the showers and stood under the hot spray. After a few minutes, McAllister came in. He had changed into his swimming trunks. They were navy blue, with two white stripes down the sides and a cord tied at the waist. He pushed the button on the shower next to Derek and stood under it, then started singing in a deep, booming voice and lathering his hairy chest with soap. Derek nudged him and giggled. After a while McAllister stopped singing and washing himself. He just stood there looking at them in a strange way, as if he was daydreaming. He moved behind them and gripped their necks in his hands.

'What have we here? Two slippery wee sticklebacks!'

They yelled and writhed out of his grip, but he didn't move away. He went on standing there behind them and started stroking their shoulders very gently with his hands. Derek looked at him, his face a cartoon of panic. McAllister's hand moved down over his chest, then he took one of his nipples between his fingers and squeezed it very gently. His other hand was doing the same with Derek. They ducked away from him and ran out of the showers, squealing and yelling as they jumped into the shallow end.

Soon it began to get busy and they noticed Shiona Fraser

with some of the other girls from school. She had a new bathing costume. A bikini. He was almost scared to look at her, but couldn't help it. She must have sensed it, because she looked at him. She even started smiling, then stopped and suddenly looked guilty about it. Derek dared him to grope her, but now that he'd grown up he knew that wasn't on, it wasn't how you should do things.

'Ah'll do it then, just watch me.'

'No you will not!'

He ducked Derek's head under the water and kept it there for a while, until McAllister, out of the showers and in uniform again, blew his whistle at him.

Derek came up gasping for air, his hair plastered over his eyes, thrashing his fists around wildly. When he got his breath he started swearing and saying he'd grope Shiona Fraser if he wanted.

'Don't you dare.'

He watched Derek climbing out of the pool and walking round to where Shiona was splashing about among the other girls. Derek jumped in beside them.

He heard their squeals and shrieks as he pushed himself away from the side as hard as he could, full of hatred for Derek. He closed his eyes and felt the water rippling under him. He moved his arms and legs angrily, then floated free for a moment before making another stroke. His foot was just about to look for the bottom when he pulled it up again and made another stroke. He was swimming. For weeks he'd been trying to learn and now he was doing it. He kept on forcing himself not to reach for the bottom with his foot, thrashing at the water with his arms and legs. He caught hold of the rail and looked up. McAllister was standing there, looking down at him. There was something not right about the look on his face. It reminded him of something. What was it? As he turned and started swimming away from him, he knew: on the bus, the way Derek had looked at the woman on the card, the way he'd looked at the gun.

On their way out, McAllister opened the door of his office and wagged a finger to tell them to come in. They shuffled in and stood there looking round the place.

'Enjoy your swim, boys?'

They nodded and said they had. McAllister looked directly at him and said:

'You can do it now, eh? I saw you. Here.'

He handed him a green card with the words 'SEASON TICKET' printed on it and told him it was his to keep.

'Thanks.'

'That's OK. Yous two are my best customers, eh? And what about you, Derek, can you do it yet?'

But he was looking at him, not Derek. He winked and added:

'Ah'm talking about swimming.'

'Nearly.'

'Ye'll soon get the hang of it. Here.'

Derek took the season ticket and said thanks. They turned to go but McAllister held up a hand to tell them to wait a minute. He looked at his feet and said:

'Don't mention it to anybody, eh? Ah mean, you can keep a secret boys, eh? These things don't grow on trees y'know.'

They looked at the green season tickets in their hands and nodded.

McAllister held out his hand to shake hands. It was such a strange thing for an adult to do, neither of them made any move. McAllister's eyebrows danced. His smile looked stuck-on.

'Come on, don't be like that, boys. You're no shakin hands wi the devil.'

*

They sat upstairs on the front seat, looking at their season tickets while the bus waited at the terminus. They still weren't speaking to each other after what had happened in the pool. After a few minutes, Derek asked:

'How come he gave us them for nothin?'

He didn't answer.

'What was he sayin "don't mention it" for?'

He gave Derek a bored look and said nothing.

'Why did he touch us in the showers?'

He held the card out in front of him and tore it in half. He put the two halves together and tore them in half again, then he put the quarters together and tore them. He scattered the torn bits of card on the bus floor.

'What did ye do that for?'

When he still didn't speak, Derek looked at his own season ticket glumly. He hesitated, then tore it up and threw the pieces on the floor with the others. After a while, he said:

'Have ye really learnt to swim?'

'Yeah. Ah did two breadths.'

Derek looked envious. Then he twisted his mouth to sneer:

'That's nothin. Ah felt between Shiona Fraser's legs.'

He wanted to punch his face for saying it, but he wanted to know what it had felt like as well. He wouldn't ask, he wouldn't ask. Derek was looking at him, a cheeky grin on his face. He was going to tell him anyway:

'It felt mouey.'

Mouey. It was one of the words you weren't allowed to write, but you could say it in the playground. It meant soft, like mud, like the mud you got down by the Esk, soft but firm, like clay. That's what mouey meant, but now it meant something else as well. It meant what it felt like between Shiona Fraser's legs. There must be more to it than that.

'How d'ye mean, "mouey"?'

Derek narrowed his eyes and looked cleverer than usual, even a bit evil.

'Like a mooth.'

Like a mooth. That was it, that was what it really meant. Imagine it. The thing between Shiona Fraser's legs was like a mouth! It was incredible to think about it.

Derek was looking pleased with himself. He couldn't let him get away with it:

'That's nothin. Ah did somethin for the first time. At the weekend.'

'What was that?'

'You know.'

It didn't take Derek long to know what he was talking about – they'd both been trying for weeks. Derek looked disappointed because he hadn't been first, then his curiosity got the better of him:

'What was it like?'

He tried to think of words to describe it, the power coming into him, his prick rearing, the hot, sticky stuff.

'It was like . . . an experience.'

Derek was impressed. It wasn't a word either of them had used before, and it sounded very adult. Derek wanted to know more:

'Was it scary?'

He nodded, then added:

'Scary but good. It was like . . .'

But all that came into his mind was McAllister sitting in his office, holding out his hand.

'. . . Like shakin hands wi the devil.'

Derek's eyes opened as wide as they could go and they stayed that way, like he was in a trance. Then he asked:

'What was the stuff like?'

'The stuff?'

He knew what Derek meant but wanted to hear him say the word. Derek looked over his shoulder to see if anyone could hear, then whispered the word in his ear.

He could say it felt hot, sticky, but he wanted to impress Derek more:

'It felt like spirit, tinder and taboo.'

Derek repeated the words softly, then he nodded slowly, as if he understood exactly what they meant. Then they both sat back in their seats and said nothing. Sometimes just the sound of words was enough, enough to make you sit back in your seat and wonder about all the things they might mean.

After a while, Derek took a packet of bubble gum out of his pocket, opened it, glanced at the card and passed the pink square of bubble gum to him. He took it, popped it in his mouth, then held out his hand for the card. He turned it over, glanced at it without really looking, then handed it back. Derek didn't even look again before squeezing it into his pocket and opening another packet. This time he just took the bubble gum out, without even bothering with the card.

The bus started up and moved off, gathering speed. He stared straight ahead at everything he could see. The road, the houses, the shops, the fields, the factories, the dark bing of the pit at Bilston, the sky . . . Everything seemed to come together into one speeding moment, rushing faster and faster towards him.

Kreativ Riting

'Today, we are going to do some writing,' says PK. 'Some *creative* writing. You do know what I mean by *creative*, Joe, don't you?'

This is what he says to me. So I says to him:

'Eh . . . Is that like when ye use they fancy letters an that?'

'No, Joe, it is not. Creative writing has nothing whatsoever to do with "they fancy letters an that",' says PK.

So I made the face like Neanderthal Man and went:

'UHHH!'

We call him PK cause his name is Pitcairn and he is a nut. So anyway, he goes round and gives everybody a new jotter each.

'For God's sake now, try and use a bit of imagination!'

Then he stops at my desk and he looks at me like I am a puzzle he is trying to work out and he says:

'If you've got one, I mean. You have got an imagination Joe, haven't you?'

This is him slaggin me, ken?

So I says to him:

'Naw, sir, but I've got a video.'

That got a laugh, ken?

So then PK says:

'The only trouble with you Joe is, your head is too chock-a-block with those videos and those video nasties. Those video nasties are worse than anything for your brain, Joe.'

Then Lenny Turnbull, who sits behind me and who is a poser, says:

'What brain? Joe's no got a brain in there, sir, just a bitty fresh air between his lugs!'

That got a laugh, ken?

So I turns round in my seat and I give Lenny Turnbull a boot in the shins, then he karate-chops me in the neck, so I slap him across his pus for him.

PK goes spare, ken?

Except nobody takes any notice, so he keeps on shouting:

'That's *enough* of that! Come on now 4F, let's have a bit of order round here!'

So then I says:

'Sir, they video nasties is no as bad as glue is for your brains but, is it?'

That got a laugh, ken?

Then Lenny Turnbull (poser) says:

'Joe's got brain damage, sir, through sniffin too much glue!'

'Glue sniffing ... solvent abuse ... is no laughing matter. Now let's have a bit of *order round here*! Right, I'm going to get you all to do a piece of writing today. You've got a whole two periods to do it in, and what I'd like all of you to do is empty your mind. In your case, Joe, that shouldn't be too difficult.'

This is PK slaggin me again, ken?

So I says for a laugh ken:

'How no, sir? I thought you said my mind was chock-a-block with video nasties?'

Then PK says:

'That's right Joe, and what I want you to do is just empty all that stuff out of your mind, so that your mind is completely blank, so that you've got a blank page in your mind, just like the one in your jotter – understand?'

'But sir, this jotter's no blank – it's got lines in it!'

'Joe, your head probably has lines in it too, through watching all those video nasties.'

Everybody laughed at that, so I made the face like Neanderthal Man again and started hitting my skull with my fist and went:

'UHHH! UHHH!'

'Joe, I knew you'd hit the headlines one day,' says PK.

Nobody laughed at that, so PK says:

'You are a slow lot today, aren't you?'

So I did the face again and went:

'UHHH!'

'Right. As I was saying before I was so rudely interrupted, what I want you to do is empty out your mind. It's a bit like meditating.'

'What's meditatin? Is that like deep-sea divin an that?' says Podge Grogan, who sits beside me.

'Not quite.'

'Of course it's no! Deep-sea divin!' says Lenny Poser Turnbull.

'Well,' says Podge, 'it coulda been! That's what it sounds like, eh Joe? Deep-sea divin in the Mediterranean an that.'

'Aye, that's right enough. Deep-sea meditatin, Ah've heard o that!'

'Away ye go! Deep-sea meditatin! Yez are off yer heids, you two!' says Lenny.

'Meditating,' says PK, 'as far as I know, has nothing to do with deep-sea diving at all, although when you think about it, the two activities could be compared. You could say that deep-sea diving and meditating are . . . similar.'

So me and Podge turns round in our seats and looks at Lenny Turnbull.

'See?' says Podge. 'Deep-sea meditatin. Tellt ye.'

'They're no the same at aw,' says Lenny. 'Ah mean, ye dinnae need a harpoon tae meditate, eh no sir?'

'Ye dae in the Mediterranean,' says Podge.

'Aye,' I says, 'it's fulla sharks an that, course ye need a harpoon.'

'Aye,' says Lenny, 'but you're talkin aboot deep-sea divin, no meditatin!'

'Well Lenny,' says PK, 'maybe you could tell the class what meditating is.'

'Aw, it's what they Buddhist monks dae.'

'Yes, but how do they do it?'

'Aw, they sit wi their legs crossed an chant an aw that.'

'Naw they dinnae,' says Podge Grogan, cause Ah've seen them. They dance aboot an shake wee bells thegither an that an sing Harry Krishner, that's how they dae it!'

'That's different,' says Lenny, 'that's no them meditatin, eh no sir?'

'Well no, I don't think so. In any case, there are different ways of meditating, but basically you have to empty your mind. You'll find it's harder to do than you think. Your mind will keep thinking of things, all the little things that clutter our minds up every day.'

'How's that like deep-sea divin, sir?' says Lenny.

'Well, it's hard to explain Lenny, I just meant that when you meditate you sort of dive into your mind, you dive into the depths of your mind and that's what I want you to try to do today. If you're lucky, you might find something there you didn't know was there.'

'Dae we get tae use harpoons?' says Podge.

'No,' says PK. 'Pens.'

Everybody goes: 'AWWW!'

'Now listen,' says PK. 'It's quite simple really. All I really want you to do is write in your jotter whatever floats into your mind. I don't want you to think about it too much, just let it flow. OK?'

'OK, PK!'

'Anything at all. It doesn't have to be a story. It doesn't have to be a poem. It doesn't have to be anything. Just whatever comes into your heads when you've emptied out your minds. Just let your mind *open up*, let the words *flow* from your subconscious mind, through your pen into your jotter. It's called Automatic Writing, and you're lucky to get a teacher like me who lets you do something like Automatic Writing, especially first two periods on a Wednesday.'

This is still PK talkin, ken. Then he says:

'I don't even want you to worry about punctuation or grammar or anything like that, just let your imagination roam free – not that you worry about punctuation anyway, you lot.'

So I says for a laugh, ken:

'Sir, what's punk–tuition? Is that like *learnin* tae be a punk?'

Everybody groaned. PK rolls his eyes and says:

'Joe, will you just shut up please?'

So I says for a laugh, ken:

'Hear that? First he's tellin us tae *open up* and now he's tellin us tae *shut up*!'

That got a laugh, ken?

Lenny Turnbull (poser) says:

'But sir, what if nothin comes intae yer heid when ye're sittin there wi yer pen at the ready?'

'Anyway, I says. 'How can I write anyway, cause I've no got a pen?'

'Use yer harpoon!' says Lenny.

'You can borrow my pen,' says PK. 'But it's more than a pen you'll need to write, Joe, because to write you also need in-spiration.'

'What's that, a new flavour o chewing gum, or what?' says Podge Grogan. So everybody starts laughin and PK goes spare again, ken. Then he brings this cassette out of his briefcase and he says:

'Right, I want you to listen to this piece of music I've got here, so that it might give you some inspiration to get you going. Just listen to the music, empty your mind, and write down whatever comes out of the music into your heads. OK?'

'OK, PK!'

'What is it, sir? Is it The Clash?'

'No, it is none of that Clash-trash. That Clash-trash is even worse for your brain than video nasties *or* glue, Joe.'

Everybody laughed, so I did the face.

'UHHH!'

'If the wind changes, your face might stay like that, Joe. Right, now stop wasting time. The music you are about to hear is not The Clash, but a great piece of classical music by Johann Sebastian Bach.'

'Who's she?' says Podge Grogan.

'*He*,' says PK, 'was a musical genius who wrote *real* music, the likes of which you lot have probably never heard before and probably won't know how to appreciate even when you do. Now I want you to be very quiet and listen very carefully to this wonderful classical piece of music and just *let go*, *let go*, and write absolutely anything the music makes you think and feel about. It's called "Air on a G string".'

'Hair on a g-string?' I says.

Everybody fell about, ken?

'Come on now 4F, let's have a bit of order round here!'

Then Lenny Turnbull says:

'But sir, can we write *absolutely* anything we want, even swearin an that?'

'Absolutely anything you want to,' says PK. 'Just listen to

the music and *let go*. I promise no member of staff will see it – except me. If you don't even want me to read it, I won't. The choice is yours. You can either read out what you've written to the class, or you can give it to me and I promise you it will be destroyed. OK?'

'OK, PK!'

Then Lenny Turnbull says:

'But sir, what about sex an that – can we put sex in it as well?'

'Hold on a minute,' says PK.

So I says for a laugh, ken:

'Hear that? First he tells us to *let go*, and now he's tellin us to *hold on*!'

That got a laugh, ken?

Then PK started clenching his fists so the knuckles went white, and he glared at me and his face went beetroot like he was ready to go completely raj.

'Look here you lot, we haven't got all day. You've wasted nearly a whole period already with your carry-on and I am sick to the back teeth of having to RAISE MY VOICE IN HERE TO MAKE MYSELF HEARD! Will you please sit *still*, keep your hands *on* the desk and YOU, Joe Murdoch, are asking for *trouble*! One more wise-crack out of you and you will be out that door and along that corridor to pay a visit to the *rector*! Do I make myself clear?'

I sort of make a long face.

'As I was saying, you may write anything you like, but I don't think this piece of music will make you think about sex, because it is not an obscene bit of music at all. In fact it is one of the most soothing pieces of music I know, so *shut up* and listen to it!'

So then PK gets the cassette machine out of the cupboard where it is kept locked up in case it walks and he plugs it in and he plays us the music. Everybody sits there and yawns.

Then Podge Grogan says:

'Sir, I've heard this before!'

'Aye, so've I!' everybody starts saying. Then Lenny Turnbull says:

'Aye! It's that tune on the advert for they Hamlet cigars!'

So then everybody starts smokin their pens like cigars and PK switches off the music.

'Put your pens *down*! Any more of this and I'm going to keep you in over the break! I am aware that this music has been used in an advertisement, but this is not the point of it at all. The point is, it was written centuries ago and has survived even until today, so *belt up and listen to it*!'

So we all sat there and listened to the music till it was finished, but nobody got any inspiration out of it at all. So then PK says:

'If anybody is stuck, you could always write something about yourself. Describe yourself as you think other people might see you. "Myself As Others See Me." Now I've got a stack of prelims to mark, so I want you to keep quiet for the rest of the time and get on with it.

So that's what I did, and here it is. This is my kreativ, autematick, deep-sea-meditatin riting:

MY OWN SELF AS OTHERS MITE SEE ME

MY NAME IS JOE MURDOCH AND I AM SHEER MENTAL SO WATCH OUT I HAVE GOT A GREEN MOHAWK IT HAS GOT SKARLIT SPIKES ON MY FOUR HEAD I HAVE GOT A SKUL AND KROSS-BONES ON MY BLACK LETHER JAKET I HAVE GOT AT LEAST 200 KROME STUDS NOT COUNTIN THE STUDS ON MY LETHER BELT AND MY DOG KOLLAR ON MY NECK I HAVE GOT A TATOO IT SAYS KUT ALONG THE DOTTED LINE ON MY

BACK I HAVE GOT NO FUTURE ON MY BOOTS I
HAVE GOT NO HOPE IN MY POCKET I HAVE GOT
NO MONEY BUT MY MUM LOVES ME AND I LOVE
HER BACK AND MY DAD STOLE THE LED OF THE
DALKEITH EPISCAPALIEN CHURCH ROOF AND I
GAVE HIM A HAND AND WE DIDNET GET
CAUGHT HA HA I AM A WARRIER AND I AM
SHEER FUCKEN MENTAL SO WATCH OUT O.K.

THE END

And now I will take out my kreativ riting to PK and tell him I
don't want to read it out to the class and I don't want him to
read it either. I will tell him I want it to be *destroyed*.

That should get a laugh, ken?

Media Studies

When he woke up, David Law heard his mum and dad moving around in the kitchen downstairs – his mum's nervous steps on the linoleum, the squeak of his dad's wheelchair – then he remembered what he'd done, and that this was the morning the *Murkirk Gazette* would come. Soon he'd have to get up, get dressed, go down and face them.

He shut his eyes and tried to get back to his dream, an erotic dream – that was the word, *erotic*, although a year ago he'd 've called it *dirty* – but now he'd lost the thread of it. Had it been about Anne, his girlfriend at school? Somehow he didn't think so. He could just remember odd bits of the dream: a white blouse and a black tee-shirt, his hand unbuttoning the blouse and moving inside it, over the black tee-shirt, then feeling the tight, firm breast with the nipple as hard as a nut, pulling the tee-shirt up, cutting open the tee-shirt with the scissors – that's right, he'd had a pair of *scissors* in the dream . . . then the short black skirt riding up over a thigh as she sat down next to him, his hand with the glue-brush in it – *glue-brush*? – reaching over and moving in there, over that black, nylon-sheathed thigh, pushing the glue-brush up into the deep, hot secret place between . . . And Jazzman just standing there watching all this going on, as if it happened every day in Media Studies.

Suddenly he remembered the face in his dream. Of course! It hadn't been Anne, his girlfriend – she was too 'nice' to be in dreams like that, and anyway she didn't get Media Studies, because she was too brainy – but another Ann, Ann Erskine.

She was in fourth year as well, but she wasn't in his class for anything except Media Studies. It was his best subject – the only subject he'd ever come top in. Last week Jazzman – his name was Mr Logan, but everybody called him Jazzman because he was always playing jazz records in his room at dinner-time – had got them all to shove the desks together in the middle of the classroom so that they could spread out the newspapers and cut out headlines and photographs from different papers and paste them in their project folders. And Ann Erskine had ended up sitting next to him. He didn't think he'd been watching her at the time – he'd never fancied her, he'd always thought she was a slag – but now he had to admit that he must've been taking it all in, because it had all been there in the dream.

Ann Erskine wore her skirts tight and short and had dyed auburn hair in a side-parting over one eye. She wore this thick black eyeliner and heavy purple eyeshadow. Her lips as well, sometimes she wore this black lipstick that made her look like something out of *The Night of the Living Dead*. She always looked sort of bored with school, as if she was thinking about something else the whole time, something else only she knew about. He had heard that she was *fast*.

Look at those *legs*, thought David, but somehow the subtitle didn't bring a picture on to the screen. What a *body*, he thought, but again the words made no movie flicker and unfold on his inner screen, his dream-screen. Maybe the projectionist had packed up and gone home, thinking there wasn't any need for another showing.

He opened his eyes and looked around the dim bedroom: that wallpaper with its repeating pattern of tanks, helicopters and ships, soldiers, pilots and deep-sea divers . . . It had been up for years and now the original blue background, a strange mixture of sky and sea, was torn in places and riddled with pin-holes and Sellotape-marks. He'd put up so many pictures of his heroes, cut from newspapers, magazines and album sleeves, then made a mess of the wallpaper when he'd taken all the pictures down again – he'd decided he didn't want to have heroes any more, that having heroes was really pretty naff.

That was one of the things he'd learnt from Jazzman, from doing Media Studies. Jazzman was always saying that hero-worship was bad for you, whether you were the worshipper or the hero. When they'd done the unit on 'Pornography in the Popular Press', about page-three girls in the *Sun* – 'Titillating Tits' he'd called his own project – Jazzman had argued with the class for nearly a whole period. Everybody had said there was nothing wrong with it, but Jazzman had said there was, because it was exploitation, not just of page-three girls, because they earned loads of money after all, but exploitation of the men who looked at them. It was encouraging grown men to worship images of women instead of caring about real women, like hero-worship except in this case the heroes were bare-breasted blondes and brunettes. That was what David liked about Jazzman – he came out with phrases like 'bare-breasted blondes and brunettes' in the class.

His mum had created hell about the mess he'd made of the wallpaper, then last week she'd started making plans to get new wallpaper, but he'd told her he didn't want any new wallpaper. He'd rather keep the room the way it was, with its massacred boy's wallpaper – it looked sort of OK like that. Then he'd told her he wanted to paint the room, and had even offered to go and buy the paint and do it himself, but there had been a raging bloody argument about the colour, because he'd wanted to paint it black. Imagine it, he'd said to Raymond King, the pal he hung about with after school, imagine it black all over, no pictures or nothing, not even one, just completely fucking *black* . . . Raymond, who still had album sleeves and posters all over his room, even the ceiling, had just shrugged and said: 'Sounds really eh . . . what's the word? Boring.' Even Raymond hadn't seen what would be pure ace about a completely black room.

He'd have to leave off about wanting to paint the walls black for a while, because this morning there was going to be another screaming row, with his mum and dad doing the shouting.

He shut his eyes again and thought about the other Ann. He still had the scissors in his hand – that was kind of weird but in a way he liked the weirdness – it made it more like a movie. The blouse, unbutton the blouse first, then feel that firm breast under the black tee-shirt, cut it open, careful, that's it . . . He didn't think she'd been wearing a bra in the dream but now he put one in anyway, a black lacy bra . . . then one snip with the scissors in the middle and it flew open. Now the glue-brush, painting the nipple with the glue-brush . . . Get down to the skirt now, cut the skirt up the front . . . He found it hard to keep the other Ann's body on the screen for very long, and even when he did it kept changing, blurring with other images he'd seen in movies, magazines and newspapers – all those 'bare-breasted blondes and brunettes'. The scissors and the glue-brush kept getting in the way as well, and sometimes Anne, his girlfriend, would barge into the fantasy and drop her schoolbag, heavy with maths and science textbooks, on the desk between him and the other Ann, then the movie would break down, the screen would go dark, there were numbers flashing across it, and in his mind David booed just the way he'd booed as a kid when the film had broken down at the Saturday matinée.

He'd seen the other Ann again this week, in the science

wing. McKenzie, the chemistry teacher, had been giving him a lecture in the corridor outside his classroom door:

'If you're no interested in the story of combustion, laddie, that's yer own look-out. There's always one, isn't there? The wise-guy, the funny man, the class cabaret. Ye think ye're hilarious, eh Law? I'll tell you something: life's no joke. Ye're a wastrel, Law, destined for the dole queue. Don't think I don't know ye've been in trouble wi the police already. It's common knowledge in the staff room. But ye'll no get away wi it in my classroom, son, ho no. An ye can sneer at a Chemistry O-level if ye like, laddie, but take it from me: without some qualifications under yer belt, you'll no go far . . .'

In the middle of it, the other Ann had come round with a circular, but McKenzie had made her stand and wait until he was finished with him. So she'd stood there listening to it all, then at one point David had looked at her and she'd looked away at the floor . . . but, yes, she'd smiled! Fuck the story of combustion, David imagined himself saying. The fantasy David then shoved McKenzie aside and swaggered off along the corridor, giving Ann Erskine a provocative glance as he passed her . . .

A clatter of dishes from the kitchen below brought him out of it. He lay completely still in the bed, listening to all the sounds from the kitchen. Sometimes he felt like he'd just arrived, just come down to the planet Earth and was seeing and hearing everything for the first time. This was what it was like now, listening to the babble of the morning news on the radio, the clatter of the cups and plates and cutlery being laid out on the kitchen table, the squeak of his dad's wheelchair, his mum's tense, high voice and the growl of his dad's answer. It was his answer to life as much as to her or what she was asking, full of scalding bitterness.

He listened to the two voices going on like that. They

sounded like water and fire. His mum's voice shook, trembled, quivered, trying to put out the crackling fire in his dad's. He wondered if their voices had always been so opposite. Maybe at one time, long ago, before the world began, water and fire had been the same substance, the same element. He tried to imagine liquid flames, but he couldn't – *If you're no interested in the story of combustion, laddie, that's yer own look-out!* – then he thought about his own voice and tried to remember how it sounded. Then he sang a few words of a song he liked – wasn't his voice like a mixture of water and fire, of his mum's voice and his dad's? He couldn't make out what they were saying to each other down there, but he knew this was the morning the paper came, that they were waiting to read about him in it, about what he'd done that Saturday night after he'd walked Anne home. They were probably talking about it now – either that or trying not to talk about it. But the not talking about it could be worse than the talking about it.

His head and his arms and his legs and his hands and his feet – in fact every part of him – felt heavy, like lead, as if it was molten lead running through his veins instead of blood. Maybe, during his sleep, he'd been paralysed. He moved his hand an inch or two under the bedclothes to make sure he wasn't paralysed, then he wondered what it would be like if he was. His dad's legs were paralysed after an accident at the foundry, and now he was living on the compensation and something called Mobility Allowance. Paralysed. The word sounded rubbery, like that rubbery sliced meat his mum sometimes bought. Half a pound of Paralysed, please. Fancy a wee Paralysed sandwich? He imagined shouting downstairs to his parents: 'Help, *help*! I'm paralysed!' That would teach them. Or if he'd been struck down in the night with some mysterious fatal illness – then they'd be sorry . . .

He pictured the gathering at his graveside: his mum having a good cry there, pushing up her glasses so as to wipe away the tears with her lipstick-smeared hanky; his dad bent double in his wheelchair, scowling with his own guilt as he threw a handful of earth on the coffin; the cops who'd arrested him both with their hats off, their walkie-talkies silent; the people in the court who'd looked him up and down and passed judgement on him; McKenzie, the chemistry-vicar, reciting the periodic table and shaking his head, praying to the God of combustion for his lower-than-O-level soul; Anne in her neat school uniform, except that now it's black, even the blouse is black, and the skirt is tight and short, like the other Ann's, and she's wearing eyeliner, black lipstick, pulling a black handkerchief out of her pencil-case . . .

He heard the clack of the letterbox, the soft thud of the paper on the hall floor, then the babble of the radio swelling as the kitchen door opened and his mum hurried out to get it.

They'd all read it. Anne's dad would read it. He was a director for a firm that manufactured, so he'd told David when he'd met him, surgical equipment – walking frames, artificial legs, things like that. David hadn't been able to help smirking about this – it was just the thought of all those plastic legs on the conveyor belt – and ever since then he'd felt her dad's disapproval when he phoned up Anne. Now he'd see that his daughter was going out with a juvenile delinquent, a criminal, and he'd forbid her to meet him. He wondered if Anne would meet him anyway, in secret, but somehow he couldn't imagine her doing that. But what about the other Ann? Maybe seeing his name in the paper would make her look at him with a new respect? It wouldn't worry her anyway, she wouldn't condemn him for it, and suddenly this seemed to David more important than anything, this not worrying and not condemning, and he wanted to talk to the other Ann more than anybody else he knew, and he swore to himself that he'd never call her a slag again, even in his thoughts. And Raymond – what would Raymond think? Raymond was doing well, he was getting good marks at school, and lately he'd been acting cool. Maybe this thing in the paper would make Raymond want to steer clear of him. And all the teachers would hand it round – *'it's common knowledge in the staff room'* – and Jazzman, what would Jazzman think of his star pupil? Maybe he'd get them to do something about it in the class, something about petty crimes and the way they were reported in the local paper, then the way more serious crimes were dealt with . . .

David wondered how his case would be reported. Maybe if there had been a spate of serious crimes, his would only get a little paragraph, hardly noticeable. But if not, there might be a headline, not a big headline of course but a headline all the same. He was curious to read about himself, about how they would describe him, but still he didn't move. How much longer could he lie here like this, not moving a muscle, para-lysed? And how could a few words printed on a piece of paper cause so much trouble, even change his life? It was the words that caused the trouble, not what he'd done.

He could imagine the little drama that would happen when he did go down. His mum, hands wet from the dishwater, wringing them dry in the dishtowel, going on about how she'd always done her best to give him a good home, how she'd worked all her life, worked her fingers to the bone, weeping and wailing that she'd never had his chance in life, his chance of a good education – and now look at what he does with it, the swine! Dragging my good name through the dirt and I don't know how I'm going to face the neighbours after this, after all we've done for you, you turn out to be a common criminal! Then his dad would get stuck in, spitting fire, jabbing at the crackling pages of the paper with his pipe, throwing the paper on the kitchen floor, roaring that he'd been roasted alive in the foundry all his life and for what? Two paralysed legs and a son who was a criminal, a criminal!

Water and fire, water and fire.

'David! Get out of your bed this minute and come down here! Your father wants to talk to you!'

He heard his dad's voice booming above the noise of the radio, a loud eruption of threats and curses. Then the kitchen door banged shut.

This was going to be the worst bit, worse than getting caught, worse than going to the court.

It'll blow over, he told himself, and he tried to think about that time to come in the future when it would have blown over, when everyone would have forgotten what he'd done, as if just by thinking about it he could magic it into now. He remembered playing the same game as a kid in the dentist's waiting room: don't listen to the noise the drills make, don't think about the injection, the pain . . . think about next Saturday, at the matinée, watching the film . . . One drill makes a high, whiney noise, the other makes a low, growling noise, but on Saturday, this Saturday coming, I am going into the pictures, I am sitting down with my bag of popcorn and my juice, the lights are going down and the curtains are opening and the film is just going to start . . . concentrate on *that!* But the noise of the drills hadn't let him imagine the film he might watch, and now his mum's voice had the same effect:

'David, get out of your bed at once!'

When the kitchen door banged shut again, he could hear her worry and her panic, even in the clatter of the plates, even in the sound of the water rattling into the kettle. It didn't matter what she was saying – he could hear the meaning. Then his dad's rumbling voice, cursing and bellowing. The two voices went on like that, clashing and interrupting each other, lamenting and condemning, as if no matter what the words were they were always saying the same things: *It's terrible, terrible! We'll just have to look on the bright side!* Then his dad's answer: *There is no bloody bright side!*

He tried to remember doing what he'd done, but now it didn't seem real, like something that had happened to somebody else a long time ago.

It had been about going away, he'd been talking to her about leaving Murkirk, going to Edinburgh, Glasgow, London, Paris, travelling the world ... but Anne hadn't been in the mood for it. She'd told him he'd get a job on a milk-float if he was lucky, the way he was going, and that after school he'd get stuck in Murkirk for the rest of his life. When he'd talked about Media Studies, trying to make it sound like something really modern and complicated, and how he might go into photography or journalism, she'd laughed and said, 'Yeah, weddings and funerals for the *Murkirk Gazette!*'

That had done it, On the way down the hill from her house – the goodnight kiss hadn't been up to much – he'd started touching the parked cars when he walked past them, then trying the doors. One had opened. He'd got in out of the cold and had sat there for a long time, just thinking about what she'd said. And she was probably right. Weddings and funerals for the *Murkirk Gazette* was the most he could hope for. It would be Anne who'd get away to university, she'd be the one who'd travel the world. He'd fiddled with things on the dashboard and had switched on the headlights, then he'd taken the hand-brake off and felt the car move forward, very slowly at first, then less slowly. He'd started to steer it, guiding it down the hill as it gathered speed, just freewheeling without the engine, that was the good thing about it, it had felt good just to be *moving*. Eventually the car slowed down and he steered it to the side of the street and put the hand–brake on. Then the cop car had drawn up alongside.

David climbed out of bed, walked over to the window and opened the curtains, then screwed up his eyes when the light hit them. Birds were singing in the back garden, and even they seemed to quarrel and accuse.

Botticelli's Flytrap

I'd only been working in the factory for a week, but every night there came a point during the shift when I could sense it out there – the darkness and silence surrounding us. Everybody else was asleep, but in here, under the strip-lights, we were making industrial ceiling tiles through the night. It was a lonely feeling, but it was a shared loneliness.

I sat on a stack of wooden pallets, doing nothing except dreaming about who I might be in the future and what I might do – rock star, artist, writer? The fantasies weren't painless – Christine always came into them somehow. If I was on stage, she was in the audience, or waiting backstage, but she was never my fan. Even in my fantasies, she was critical of my performances and making her own demands. If I was an artist or a writer – she might be a model or a muse, but I knew her too well to think she'd be flattered by some daubs on a canvas, or something called 'Love Poem'. Maybe that was why I liked her.

We'd split up during my first year at university. Now she'd finished school as well and was working for the summer in a hotel somewhere in the Highlands. I couldn't imagine her doing kitchen work. It didn't fit my idea of her – someone almost mythically beautiful.

Work seemed to have ground to a halt. I had no idea why and didn't feel like asking. If I did, somebody might give me something to do, like cleaning the Riddle – the huge machine that punched all the holes in the sheet metal before it was guillotined and shaped into ceiling tiles. I was dead scared of the Riddle. Operating it was like walking up and down inside a huge engine, the engine of a ship maybe, with these narrow walkways between the pistons and the wheels and the blades. Most of the safety guards were broken or loose or missing altogether. Sometimes Rab – the apprentice who worked alongside me – poked fun at my caution. I was always for stopping the machine when we had to remove 'slugs' – bits of stuff that got on to the sheet metal and made dents in the tiles. He could poke fun all he wanted. I still wasn't sure what I wanted to be, but I knew I didn't want to be an industrial ceiling tile.

Nearby, at the work-bench they used for their piece-time, three of the men were playing cards. Beside me, on a heap of old rags, Rab slept or pretended to, curled up under an oil-stained overall, his boots sticking out one end and his black, close-cropped hair out the other. I opened my haversack. Between my piece-box and my flask, both empty now, was *The Story of Art*. I tugged the book out and lowered the haversack to the floor. I'd failed the first year exam in the History of Art. I had to pass the re-sit or I'd be out on my ear.

I opened the book and looked at some of the pictures, trying to memorize names and dates. Rab suffered from asthma – he'd failed the medical for the army – and every so often the rasp of his breathing distracted me. Either that or it was the shouts of the men playing cards. The factory lighting wasn't good for reading, and sometimes the print blurred and seemed to move around on the page. I found myself staring at Botticelli's Venus again. She didn't really look like Christine, but somehow she reminded me of her. Maybe it was her expression or the look in her eyes – but no, it was something I couldn't pin down. The picture filled me with a kind of hopeless longing.

I looked up when I heard the men cheering and clapping. Sammy the gatehouse attendant had come in with the wage packets. He carried them in what looked like a shoe-box, and he'd put the box down on the table to clean his glasses with his hanky. I shook Rab's shoulder and told him our wages had arrived. He sat up and pretended to be waking from a deep sleep, stretching and yawning. I shut the book, jumped down from the pallets and walked over to the table where the men were. Rab followed me.

'Here comes Brian and his gang,' said Archie McGlone, grinning. Every time he grinned he exposed the gap between his eye-teeth where he'd taken his dental plate out. A lot of the men seemed to work without their teeth in on the night shift. Was it just because they were used to taking them out at night, or because there were no women on?

It was a question.

Mick McIver was the same, except with him it was the complete set of falsers, top and bottom. He kept them wrapped in a dirty rag in his boiler-suit pocket.

'Yous two are no gettin peyd,' he said. 'Ye're too fuckin lazy.'

'Listen tae whae's talkin,' said Sammy. 'McIver the skiver.'

McIver's laughter was a harsh bark of derision, then he spat out:

'Fuck off ya miserable four-eyed cunt ye. Every time Ah pass that gatehoose ye've got the feet up, daein the fuckin crossword!'

'Aye, either that or he's studyin page three!' said Archie McGlone, working his eyebrows up and down, grinning and making his eyes dart from one side to the other. He looked like a ventriloquist's dummy.

'Aye, that'll be right,' said Sammy, then he shook his head, looked at me and Rab and blew some air out of his mouth in a display of disgust.

I got the feeling that this banter was for my benefit.

Sammy put his glasses on squintly, picked up the shoe-box and sorted through the pay packets importantly.

I put *The Story of Art* face down on the table and sat on a metal crate. I shifted along a bit, reluctantly, to make room for Rab.

Since I'd come to the factory, Rab had latched on to me. He followed me around, sat beside me at piece-time, and usually ended up working with me. Maybe it was just because I was the only other guy under twenty. At first I'd felt glad of the company. Then I'd felt sorry for him – most of the men in the factory seemed to treat him with contempt, or pity. Now I was beginning to feel impatient with his loyalty and wanted to shake him off.

'Awright boys?' said Jake Dunnigan, then he licked the paper of the cigarette he was rolling with exaggerated care. He was a lean, handsome man who always carried a comb in the back pocket of his jeans. His hair was slicked back and the collar of his donkey jacket was usually turned up. He was very much in charge of himself.

Mick shuffled the cards, nodded at me and Rab and said to him:

'Look at the paira them. Tweedle-fuckin-dee an Tweedle-fuckin-dum!'

Jake raised an eyebrow, lit up and half-closed his eyelids in a show of mild amusement. He didn't let himself laugh very often. He was very controlled, but he gave me the feeling that if he ever lost control, chances were he wouldn't find it again till it was time to plead guilty.

His face was pale, pinched. His lips were thin, tight. If you asked him for the time, he'd look you in the eye very seriously before glancing at his watch and telling you. It was like you'd asked him something deeply personal.

McIver was different. He was liable to boil over at the least wee thing. Some of the men in the machine shop called him Mad Mick. On my first night, Archie McGlone had warned me about him. He'd called him a cowboy, a chancer, a heidbanger. I'd expected a young guy, but he was in his late fifties. In a way that added an edge to the reputation – he was still wild. He wore a dirty old mud-coloured polo-neck under his boiler-suit. His skin was leathery, as if he'd worked outside a lot. He probably had. He had a pug nose and sleekit-looking green eyes. He'd done some amateur boxing when he was younger. I'd heard he was still doing it – but not in the ring.

'Righto boys,' said Sammy. 'The moment yous have all been waitin for.'

'No hauf,' said Archie McGlone.

'Get on wi it, ya bumptious wee nyaff ye,' said Mick McIver.

Sammy rounded his eyes in outrage at this latest insult, then called out our names briskly as he threw us our wage packets. The men opened them, took out the pay-slips and studied them. I did the same. It was my first wage packet, and I couldn't help smiling with real pleasure when I saw the folded notes inside. I hadn't held so much cash in my hand for a long time.

When Sammy had gone, Mick leered at Jake, hammered the side of his fist on the workbench, held out his wage packet, shook it up and down and declared:

'Get a ride the night, eh?'

Archie McGlone grinned and said:

'Ah get yin anywey.'

'Aw? Lucky cunt you. Ah suppose she's lyin there waitin for ye every mornin wi the suspenders on, is she?'

'Oh aye, definitely, that's right!'

Archie was grinning and rubbing his hands together furiously.

'Ye're a fuckin liar McGlone. Ah bet ye're lucky if she puts the kettle on for ye.'

'Wid ye lissen tae yersels,' said Jake. 'Should be ashamed o yersels talkin like that in front o these young boys.'

'Away ye go,' said Mick. 'This yin's probly gettin it every night up at the Uni. That yin's too saft in the heid tae ken whit we're on aboot!'

'Ah might be saft in the heid, but that's no what counts,' said Rab.

'Stoap that, ya rajie wee bastard ye,' said Jake, then he looked down at my lap and added: 'An you mind an keep yon thing in yer troosers up at the Uni.'

I smiled uneasily. Since the split with Christine, my first year had passed without any chance to take it out. I wasn't making contact in other ways as well. One of my tutors had put his finger on it when he'd said to me: 'If you don't want to come to classes, that's up to you, but for heaven's sake *have a good time!*' I wasn't doing either. I wasn't fitting in. I felt intimidated by some of the other students, who seemed to know so much about art already. It was like I was in a foreign country and didn't speak the language.

Mick shuffled the cards, slammed them on the table and took a half bottle of whisky from somewhere inside his boiler-suit. He unscrewed it quickly, took a swig, then offered it to Jake. Jake looked over his shoulder to the door into the machine shop, then wiped the bottle and took a drink. Archie McGlone said he couldn't trust himself to take a drink at this time of the night. Mick laughed at this derisively. Rab wasn't even considered. He offered the bottle to me.

I didn't want the drink, but I didn't want to turn it down either. I took it and tried to look as if I'd done this before, but the whisky made me wince. Archie and Mick roared with laughter. Mick thumped me on the back as he took the bottle out of my hand. He had another swig, drinking so much that his Adam's apple moved up and down in his throat. He smacked his lips and rolled his toothless jaws around, his eyes narrowing like a cat's, then he tucked the bottle back into his boiler-suit and said:

'Gie ye a tip, son – see whisky? Sometimes when ye've been drinkin whisky, ye can ride aw night. Ither times ye cannae even get it up – that right, Jake?'

Jake, who was humming a tune to himself and smoking with a preoccupied air, glanced at me and said:

'Aye, that's yin o life's great mysteries, right enough.'

'Take the pish if ye like,' said Mick. 'Fuckin true though.'

Archie McGlone offered me his tuppence-worth:

'Dinnae listen tae him. You get yersel a guid wee wife, son. She'll look efter ye. If ye feel like a bitty the ither, ye dinnae have tae gawn oot lookin for it. Ye juist gawn ben the room. If ye feel like a bevvy, ye can ayewis huv a few cans put by in the fridge.'

'Aye an ye can even ask her fuckin permission tae drink yin,' said Mick, cowering and clasping his hands together in a parody of the henpecked husband begging for a can of beer.

Jake almost laughed. But it wasn't real. It was like somebody saying: 'I am laughing. I think that is very funny.'

Mick was watching Jake closely. He sniffed up his phlegm, stood up, put his pay packet in his pocket and announced:

'Ah'm away for a pish.'

When Mick had gone, Jake turned over *The Story of Art* and opened it. He flicked through the pages casually, tilting his head a little as he looked at the pictures. The book happened to fall open at the picture I'd looked at most.

'Whit d'ye cry this yin?'

'Eh . . . That's Botticelli's Venus.'

'Nice wee paira tits on her.'

Archie threw his head back and gave out a gargling laugh. Jake turned his head in Archie's direction very slowly and gave him a withering look. The gesture seemed to take ages. He opened his mouth, then he spoke:

'What the fuck's funny, McGlone? Ah suppose you're the tits expert round here.'

'Aye,' said McGlone. 'Ah've seen better in *Playboy*.'

'Ye mean bigger, is that what ye mean?'

'Aye. The bigger the better, eh boys?'

Rab dug me in the ribs with his elbow and laughed a low laugh. I didn't join in. He was really bothering me.

'Shows how much you know aboot art,' said Jake. He flicked through the book and stopped to look at another picture. He raised an eyebrow and gave a low whistle. Archie leaned over to look.

They had their heads together, these grown men, to look at the masterpiece, as if it was a rare kind of pornography they hadn't come across before.

Jake turned the picture to me and said:

'What's this yin cried?'

It was one of the paintings I'd failed to identify in the exam, and I still couldn't. If I was put in a corner, I'd probably have plumped for a title like 'The Rape of Lucretia'.

'I think it's a Titian.'

'The tits are nothin tae right hame aboot. Some arse on her though, eh?'

'Aye, that's mair like it,' said Archie, nodding and grinning. 'Ah wouldnae kick her oot o bed.'

Jake looked at me and winked.

'Away ye go McGlone, she'd eat ye for breakfast, eh boys?'

'She can have me for breakfast any day,' said Rab.

Jake left it to Archie to tell me to tell Rab to shut up.

Mick came back in buttoning up his boiler-suit and whistling. When he came up to the table, he leaned over Jake's shoulder to look at the book.

'Whit's this – pornography?'

'Naw, it's art,' said Archie. 'Here Mick, which yin dae you fancy, the tits-yin or the botty-what's-it?'

Jake flicked through the pages to find the Botticelli. When he did, Rab stuck his head in front of the picture and said:

'Reminds me o that wee burd in the paint-shop. Sandra somethin.'

Archie looked at Rab askance.

'Sandra Purves? You have got to be jokin! Some Venus her, eh?'

'Aye,' said Mick. 'A fuckin Venus flytrap!'

Rab grinned sheepishly as the men laughed at him.

Mick looked at Botticelli's Venus briefly and said:

'Naw. Ah've met her type. Fuckin prick-teaser. Let's see the ither yin again.'

Jake turned the pages to the Titian, if it was a Titian.

'She's the yin for me,' said Mick. 'Ah like a bitty meat.'

'Tellt ye,' said Archie to Jake.

Jake shook his head at the others' lack of taste and said:

'It's the tits we're talkin aboot. Which yin's got the nicer paira tits?'

Mick sat down, spat in his hands and rubbed them together. His tongue wriggled between his toothless gums, his eyes narrowed, then he said:

'It's no the tits ye ride.'

Jake agreed with this very seriously, as if Mick had made a very profound point. Archie grinned, then the grin soured on his face and he nodded his head and said:

'Aye, right enough.'

Jake went on looking at pictures. After a minute, Archie said:

'Put that book away afore Ah get too excited.'

'Ye've probly got a hard-on already McGlone,' said Mick.

'So? What if Ah dae?'

'It's no meant to gie ye a hard-on,' said Jake. 'It's art, eh?'

He looked to me for confirmation.

I shrugged and nodded.

Jake went on flicking through the pages, stopping to study a nude every so often. At one point Mick grabbed the book from him and pointed at a photograph of a Greek statue of the god Mars.

'How come they've aw got totty wee wullies?'

I didn't know. It wasn't a question that had come up in any of the tutorials I'd got to.

'Must've been an awfy cauld mornin,' said Archie, then he gargled on his own laughter loudly.

'Ye should ask yer fuckin teacher,' said Mick, throwing the book on the workbench with contempt.

'Heh. Watch the boy's book, eh?' said Jake. He turned the book over and opened it respectfully.

'Ah used tae draw a bit masel, but Ah didnae have the talent. This cousin o mine, Eddie, he had it. He could look at that picter an draw that Venus, the exact same thing, perfect. Frae memory tae. Telln ye. He could dae thon whit d'ye cry it. Laughin Cavalier — is that yin in here?'

I shook my head and said I didn't think so.

Jake looked disappointed. He took a long draw on his cigarette, blew the smoke out like a sigh, then looked at me very seriously and said:

'You stick in, son. You learn aboot art an that. Learn yersel a foreign language — Italian, French, Spanish and that. Then ye can fuck off away frae this dump. No like us. We're fuckin stuck here.'

Mick was shuffling the cards impatiently.

'Ach stoap puttin ideas in the boy's heid ya daft cunt ye.'

Jake clenched his jaws and looked at Mick steadily.

'Who're you callin a cunt?'

'If ye think the boy's gonnae be better off ower there, in Italy or Spain or some fuckin place, ye must be a daft cunt. It's the fuckin same everywhere. Them an us. As for learnin aboot art – what the fuck use is that gonnae be tae him? What kinda job's he gonnae get wi a degree in aw that fuckin stuff? Answer me that.'

But Jake decided Mick wasn't worth answering. He said to me:

'Dinnae listen tae that ignorant bastard.'

Before he could say any more, Mick flung the pack of cards on the table so violently that they scattered everywhere. He was up on his feet and stabbing at the air with a finger and shouting:

'Call me an ignorant bastard, wid ye? It's yersel ye're talkin aboot ya cunt ye. Art, by fuck – tryin tae tell us aboot art? You donno fuck-all aboot it Dunnigan so don't fuckin come it!'

Jake's face was pale, his mouth tight, his knuckles white. Without taking his eyes off Mick, he began to rise from his seat slowly. Suddenly Archie was on his feet, one hand on Jake's shoulder, the other held up to Mick, his grin now a grimace of fear. He danced around frantically between them.

'Aw c'mon now boys, cool it. This is no the time or the place, we're no gonnae fight ower a fuckin art book, c'mon now, dinnae be silly—'

He went on saying things like that, all the time gesticulating and pulling faces, until Mick sat down again.

Archie tried to make a joke of it all as he gathered the scattered cards together:

'See aw the trouble ye've caused? Ye come in here frae yer

Edinburry University wi yer fancy books on art history and yer big ideas an see whit happens—'

Mick snatched the cards from Archie's hand and began to shuffle them.

'Aw shut it McGlone,' he said.

'Aye, button it,' said Jake.

Rab dug me in the ribs with his elbow, rolled his eyes and let out a soft, low whistle.

'Right,' said Mick. 'Put the fuckin art gallery away an let's have a game. Fancy a wee game o pontoons boys?'

I took the book and put it on the floor beside my feet.

'Count me out,' said Rab.

'Surprise surprise.'

'What aboot you, Brian?'

It was the first time Mick had called me by my name. It felt good to take the money out of my own wage packet and toss it into the kitty with an air of contempt like the others. Rab was my supporter, and every so often he'd blow on one of the cards I was given for luck. More often than not, this seemed to bring the card bad luck, and after a while I stopped him doing it. Then he looked so sad that I relented and let him blow on a card. If I won, he cheered. When I lost, he commiserated with me. It didn't matter if I won or if I lost. I was playing, that was what mattered.

Conversation dwindled, and time seemed to congeal around the card game. I was drawn into the repetition and the boredom of it – it was a new kind of boredom for me, and it was irresistible.

Later, I sat with Rab on the prongs of a fork-lift, drinking tea from paper cups. Rab had gone to the tea-machine and brought them back for us. I had opened the book and was turning the pages, but Rab didn't seem to take the hint.

'How much did he skin ye?'

'Not much. A few quid.'

'See when Jake Dunnigan started gettin up – Christ! Ah wis like that.'

He held out his hand and made it shake.

'Ah wis sure they were gonnae thump the shit oot each other. Were you no?'

I shrugged and drank some tea. Rab shook his head, imagining what had almost taken place. After a moment, he went on:

'Aw because o yon book! They nude picters! Fuckin mental, so it is!'

'Yeh, mental.'

There was a long silence between us. I turned a few pages and stopped again at Botticelli's Venus. It still made me think of Christine, except that now Jake and Mick's voices were getting in the way: *Nice wee paira tits on her. Fuckin prick-teaser*. Rab finished his tea, then crunched up the cup in his hand, threw it on the floor and stamped on it with his boot. Suddenly he looked at me and asked:

'You winchin, or what?'

I shook my head and sent the question back to him. Rab nodded and beamed, hardly able to contain his pride.

'We're gettin engaged.'

'Is that right? When?'

'Soon as Ah've saved up enough for the ring.'

'Congratulations, Rab. Nice, is she?'

'Aye. Better lookin than her any day.'

A dismissive nod at Botticelli's Venus.

When he asked me if there was nobody I even fancied, I told him about the split with Christine. When I'd finished, he asked:

'Still love her, dae ye?'

I shrugged, opened my mouth to answer but couldn't. Rab was watching me, and he came to my rescue:

'Mibbe yez'll get back thegither then.'

I wanted to be on my own to think about that. I shut the book, finished my tea, then told Rab I was going for a smoke and walked to the back door of the factory.

Outside, I leaned against the factory wall and smoked. A train sped by – the overnight train from London, heading north. I tried to fantasize about Christine: those wondering blue eyes, that coppery red hair of hers, her lips parting in the prelude to a smile . . . it was the same picture I'd often painted in my mind, but now it seemed different. I realized it had become a memory.

I looked at the huddle of dark houses on the other side of the reservoir. One of those houses was mine, my mum and my dad were sleeping there, it was where I was from. I tried to make it out, but it was still too dark. If I waited a bit longer, until it was light, maybe then I'd be able to see it.

Peninsula

When she was rinsing out her cup at the sink Mary McAfferty, the cleaner, looked out the window of the staff room and down the street to her front door. She saw the door opening and Ernie coming out of the house. She watched him limping down the path and along the street. Because of his bad leg he had to keep stopping to rest. He stood there, leaning on his walking stick and tilting his head to the side, like he was listening to the pain in his leg. Hunched in his old coat, his cap drooping over one eye, he reminded her of a mole trying to find its way in the daylight. After his years down the pit, maybe he'd got used to being under the ground. She watched him limp away down the street, grasping at the wall with his hand, determined to get where he was going. She knew where that was – he'd cross the road after the railway bridge, go along past the cemetery and bury himself in the Digger's Arms till it shut for the afternoon.

Hell mend him.

What a morning. Usually, on a holiday, she'd get the place spick-and-span, get the things done she didn't get the time for usually. There was never the time to get everything done. Polishing the doorhandles with a bit of Brasso. Giving the floors a right good scrub. Not the day though.

She'd spent the first two hours in the boys' toilets. Bad buggers the lot of them. If they were hers she'd leather their behinds for them. Imagine it. Smearing their shit all over the walls. Sheer badness. Never in all her years as a cleaner had she been asked to clean up such a thing. She'd cleaned houses, stairs, hospitals, offices, cinemas and now the primary school. It was part-time but it was always something. The extra money came in handy, what with Ernie on a disability pension because of his leg and Paul up at the university.

She put on her rubber gloves and gave the sink a quick rub round with a bit of Jif. The clean smell of it helped her to forget that other smell. Just thinking about it was enough to scunner you. In her day, such a thing could never have happened, it would have been unthinkable. Nobody would have even thought of doing an unthinkable thing like that. There was something far wrong with the world nowadays.

She took off the gloves and put them on the draining board. Just the classroom to do now. She turned to the little mirror beside the sink, pulled the lipstick out of her housecoat pocket and put some on. She took a paper towel from the dispenser and pressed her mouth on it, then crumpled it up and put it in the bin. She put the lipstick away and looked at herself again, made small adjustments to her hair – more grey than black. Time for another sachet of Harmony. She straightened her glasses and opened her big, hazel-coloured eyes wide and tried on a smile. Then she said something to the face in the mirror:

'Who're you kiddin?'

She took her brush and her duster along the corridor and into the classroom and started on the floor. Damned if she was going to scrub or mop it after this morning. A quick sweep and nobody would be any the wiser.

She went on sweeping the floor for a few minutes, then stopped and let the handle of the brush fall its length on the floor. She stood completely still for a minute, then the hand that had been holding the brush dropped to her side and her whole body began to sag. She sat down on one of the tiny wooden desks and felt the feeling come over her. Like a fountain of lead, sprouting from her heart and flooding her body to her fingertips and lips and eyes.

She had better get on. She didn't have to think about the work, all she had to do was do it. Today was different though. Today her hands felt heavy and useless, and she couldn't bring herself to pick up the fallen brush and go on. She was completely and utterly browned off. She felt she could almost greet. She took off her glasses, then blew her nose noisily. Now that she'd sat down she was going to have a smoke and that was that. She fished in the pocket of her housecoat for her fags and her lighter. As she smoked, she stared at the blurred word chalked on the blackboard. Then she put her glasses back on and read it. It said:PENINSULA. Everything else had been rubbed out.

She was caught coming out of the paper-shop by auld Mrs Logan the lollipop woman. The usual complaints about the weather. It was too close and it was giving her trouble with her breathing. On her day off as well – as if the weather should have taken that into account. Then it was Paul – had he had his exam results yet? Neither had Davy, her laddie – he was doing engineering at the Heriot Watt – but he'd got an interview for a job the next week.

Mary smiled and nodded and said that was very good.

'What's it your Paul's daein again?'

'Philosophy.'

'Oh aye, that's it. Ah'm aye forgettin. Ah don't suppose there's many jobs in philosophy these days, is there?'

'Well, we'll see. He might find something.'

'Aye, ye see whit it is, there's no the demand for philosophers like what there used tae be.'

'Mibbe not, but he might be lucky.'

'Aw aye, ye never know.'

'Well, Ah'd better away Mrs Logan—'

That woman. Always on about how great her laddie was getting on at the Heriot Watt. Always asking her what it was Paul did and then going on about the demand for philosophers. As if she knew the first thing about it. Not that she knew much about philosophy herself, although she was aware of the spiritual dimension – she read her stars religiously in the paper every day and had recently joined the Rosicrucians. Their magazines were well produced, it had to be said, compared to some of them.

She was hardly in the door when the phone went. It was Paul saying he was coming on the five o'clock bus. She asked him what he wanted for his tea. Anything. Why did they never give you more warning? They just landed on you, but what could you do?

Ernie, damn him, came back from the pub. She told him Paul was coming and he went upstairs for a lie down.

When he was out of the way, she made herself a cup of tea and sat down and put her feet up and had a smoke and read her horoscope. It said somebody very close to her would act distant, or else she was to expect a visit from a dark stranger. What could that mean – Paul? She read his. It said he had to stop running away from his responsibilities and face up to life. It said a member of the opposite sex would surprise him with some unexpected news. She'd suspected as much. It meant he wasn't doing his studying. And if that girlfriend of his got herself pregnant it would put the tin lid on it.

She read the TV page but her mind wasn't on it, she was worrying herself sick about Paul. He'd be back at half-five. She'd have to feed him. She'd make him chips for his tea. He liked chips. She had some bacon and some black pudding and she could always fry him an egg and a bit of fried bread. Or maybe she'd go up to the Co-op and get some liver. She could fry it with an onion. Paul would eat that, and Ernie had always liked a fried onion.

The smell of they ingins is gawn straight to ma heart. That's what he'd said to her the first time she'd cooked his dinner for him after they'd got married. They'd lived in Craigmillar then, and he'd worked in Whitehill Colliery in Rosewell. It had been a hard time, especially when the first two bairns had been born, but he had work. There had been the times he'd got overtime on a Sunday. He'd used an old bike to get to work because there was no bus early enough on the Sunday morning. A twelve-hour shift, and after it he'd had to cycle the eight miles back to Craigmillar. When he got in he was that tired he could barely speak, he could barely eat the meal she'd made for him. Unless the conductor let him take the bike on the bus, that sometimes happened, and he'd be that bit less tired when he got in and the bairns would sing and dance and clap their hands because he'd got back early.

The trouble with a man like Ernie was that he frittered money away. He didn't save. He had no idea of bettering himself. He had wasted his life with politics and reading books and drinking and betting. It was a downright shame when you thought about it, a man with his brains.

It was when he got politics that the real trouble had started. Making an arse of himself in public. Up on the stage at the miners' gala day. Standing for election for the communist party. Some of they other wide-boys were laughing at him up their sleeves. Ernie hadn't been able to see that he was being taken for a ride. The upshot was that he was found guilty along with the rest of them. Embezzling the gala day funds. She'd had to take in sewing and go out scrubbing stairs to pay the fine.

It was funny how she'd been having a lot of these memories lately, along with the heavy feeling sprouting inside her. Miller had said it was just her time of life. Maybe if she went back to see him he'd give her something for it. Either that or she could go to the chemist and get another bottle of that Yeast-vite.

She looked at the clock on the mantelpiece. It was that time already and she hadn't even started on the papering. She hurried through to the kitchen, put on her housecoat, cleared the table and started. She mixed up a bucket of wallpaper paste and got the rolls of paper out the cupboard. She'd a couple of lengths cut and ready to hang so she could get started right away. When the paste had set she spread it on the first length of paper with the brush, then gathered it up and carried it into the hall. She'd forgotten to put the steps up! She had to go back into the kitchen and lay the paper down carefully, then get the steps out the meter cupboard. At last she was up on the steps, smoothing out the paper, making sure the pattern was matching, creasing it at the top and the bottom and trimming it with the shears.

It was good work, better than cleaning, because at the end of the day you had something to show for it, not that it made a blind bit of difference to him. The first time she'd wallpapered after they'd got married, it had become crystal clear to her that her man was handless. He did not have a clue when it came to matching a repeating pattern. She had sent him out and had finished the job herself. Since then, every time the house was decorated, he'd made himself scarce. Even when they flitted, he went away out for the day and came back to a different house. Imagine that! Once, she remembered, the bairns had turned his chair upside down to see if he would notice and he'd just walked in and sat down quite the thing on the settee!

All the houses they'd lived in. At least twenty. She'd decorated and then redecorated, then flitted and started decorating again – that was a repeating pattern as well! Funny when you thought about it, all that wallpapering and painting she'd done over the years – and that many flittings! And here she was papering again, at her age, although one thing she would not be doing again was flitting. Mind you, it would be nice to afford a beautiful home, but you just had to do the best with what money you had. This was it, this was the thing.

She heard him getting out his bed and going to the bathroom so she trimmed the bit she was putting up and stopped and cleared the stuff away. It was time to get the tea on anyway, Paul would be in any minute.

He came down and started getting under her feet, wanting to hear the news on the radio and wanting a cup of tea while he read the paper. It was news, news, news all day with Ernie. Starting with the early news on the radio, right through the day. It would make you sick, so it would, all that news, but what could you do? You just had to grin and bear it.

She'd just got the chips on when Paul came in the back door. There was something far wrong with him, she could tell that at a glance. He looked like something the cat had brought in. That hair of his – what like was it? And thin? He couldn't be eating right. She hoped he wasn't on drugs or anything like that. You heard so many stories.

When she got the food laid out and sat down at the table, Ernie started making his cracks but she ignored them. It was good to see Paul eating, but she could tell he wasn't that hungry. He'd barely touched his black pudding. Then they started arguing about Russia and what was happening in one of they other countries near Russia. It was always the same with the two of them these days – politics.

After his tea he fell asleep on the couch. She looked at him lying there wearing his jeans and his tee-shirt. It stirred her up inside to see him lying there sleeping like one of they Greek gods. That girlfriend of his – did she appreciate him? She doubted it. She was a silly wee lassie from Sussex, who had once had the effrontery to say that she, Mary, was a blether.

When they went out to the club she watched her programme in peace, then she finished off the papering. When it was done she put the steps back in the meter cupboard and cleared everything away and got herself ready for the morning. Then she looked at the hall. It looked nice, clean and fresh, and most of the roses matched perfectly. Nobody would really notice the bits that were out of line. Nobody except her. It would be a while till they came back, so she made herself a cup of tea and put her feet up and watched the film, but it was an old film she'd seen before a long time ago.

She was nodding off in her chair when the pair of them came in and she had to get up and make them some tea and some cheese on toast. She could hear them talking in the living room as she watched the grill. They were arguing again. When she went through they were still at it. This time it was that carry-on in Czechoslovakia.

She tried to change the subject:

'How are you getting on at the university?'

A shrug.

'What about your flat?'

'What about it?'

'Is it warm enough?'

'Aye, Mum.'

'What are you eating?'

Paul waved a bit of toast in the air.

'Cheese on toast.'

'I'm no talking about that. I mean are you feeding yerself right in Edinburgh?'

Another shrug. He looked that serious, especially with they

specs he wore. You couldn't tell what he was thinking half the time, and when you asked him all you got was an aye or a no, or a shrug, and that was that.

Her horoscope had hit the nail on the head. Somebody close acting distant. It was like that. It was like your laddie went away to the university and a stranger came home. There was something wrong but he wouldn't let on what it was. Maybe he didn't know what it was hisself.

When they started shouting at each other – politics again – she felt the heavy feeling inside, like something overflowing and flooding her insides.

'Stop it, please! Listen to yersels, worse than them up in the House of Commons!'

They both had a laugh at that, and that only made her feel worse:

'Neither of you even noticed the hall! I've been papering it all day! This morning, I had to clean up *shit*—'

She hadn't meant to mention it, but now that she had, the story of her day came out in a confusion of words and tears. She couldn't help herself any longer.

They were that surprised, the pair of them, that they both got up off their chairs and then just stood there looking at her like they didn't know what to do next.

Then Paul went into the kitchen to get her a cup of coffee.

'Ye should've refused! Ye should've tellt that heidmaister tae dae it hissel! Ah'll be up at the schule the morn – Ah'll kick up hell!'

She told him no, that was the last thing she wanted, she just wanted peace, she just wanted no arguments about politics and whatnot in her own house. Then she told him he hadn't even noticed the new wallpaper in the hall and he said of course he had and that it made a difference. Then he shut up and turned up the TV – news again – and asked if there was any more tea. She went through to the kitchen and saw Paul sitting there looking at the table waiting for the kettle.

She wanted to ask him what the matter was, but you couldn't just come out with it just like that. She busied herself around him, then, because she wanted to ask him something, said:

'What does "peninsula" mean?'

He looked up, surprised. Then he stared at her and spoke like he was reading out of a book:

'A peninsula is a narrow strip of land, projecting from the mainland into the sea. A peninsula is almost an island.'

She felt glad she'd asked, and thought of something else:

'Is Scotland a peninsula?'

The way he stared at her when she asked that made her think she'd asked something difficult, something important.

'In a way it is, but "peninsula" also has another meaning, Mum.'

She sat down at the table with him to hear it.

'A peninsula is also a time in a person's life when they feel alone but not free, when they feel like a stranger among friends. They feel they don't really belong, but can't break away from where they are.'

'Fancy that.'

'A peninsula is a very difficult time for some people, Mum. Sometimes they get over it, sometimes they don't and the peninsula goes on until they die.'

'Fancy them teaching them that at primary school.'

'Maybe it was the first meaning they were teaching them, Mum.'

'Even so.'

She got up and filled the teapot and let it infuse, then she looked at him. He was sitting there with his head in his hands, shaking, like he was starting to greet. She laid her hand lightly on his shoulder. She was just going to ask him if that was what was wrong with him, if he was having a peninsula, when lo and behold, she saw that he was laughing. He took his hands away from his face and threw his head back and laughed and laughed and laughed. He was laughing but he wasn't happy. It was like watching a stranger laughing. She'd never seen the like of it before.

Whatever it was, there was definitely something very far wrong with him.

I'm Glad That Wasn't Me

The taxi shuddered as Gus paid the driver and waited for the receipt. Gus shuddered with it as he looked through the tinted glass at the down-and-out: he stood on the corner scratching his itches, grinning at nothing with tobacco-tinted teeth, shifting his weight from one bow leg to another, trying to trap a passer-by between the separate stares of his wall-eyes. Every day he was there, dressed in the same ripped and stained rags he'd been wearing since he'd first shown up on the street – his legs and back buckled as if by a great weight, an endless labour. His face and hands and bald scalp were burnished red, as if he'd been boiled alive like a lobster, or baptized in fire. At the same time he looked clownish – swaying from side to side as he walked, eyes askew. One day last week, when he'd turned the corner into the street, Gus had been troubled by the tramp's elongated shadow falling across his path like a bad omen.

The tramp had been coming into his restaurant almost every day for the past two weeks, a disarming grin smeared across his face, smacking his tobacco-flecked coins on the counter and requesting a pot of tea for one. Gus had put up with him, and there was no real reason not to: the man was polite, more civil than many of the regulars. He took his tray with its pot, its tea-strainer, its little jug of milk and its cup and saucer to a table in the corner, where he sat for an hour or so smoking if he had anything to smoke and contemplating his image in the wall-mirror. One day he'd sat there puffing away at a fat cigar, and though he'd no doubt cadged it from someone on the street, in a burlesque way the cigar had suited him. On other days, Gus'd suspected the guy of falling asleep.

Who was he? Where did he come from? More to the point: when would he go away? Things were definitely getting worse in the street.

When the driver handed him the receipt Gus opened the door farthest away from where the down-and-out stood and crossed to the other pavement. Even so he thought he heard the man calling out behind him – a polite 'excuse me'. The politeness sounded practised – a kind of irony.

He decided not to hear him and hurried along the street. He was late, and already one or two of the dealers were opening up. In the last year or two the street had become infested with antique shops, displaying in their windows few genuine antiques – it was mostly old sideboards and dressers, sanded and varnished, and the odd grandfather clock that didn't work. Some of the humblest household objects from his childhood were now, apparently, sought-after items: old biscuit tins, clockwork toys.

Maybe, instead of opening a restaurant, he should have gone into junk, but he doubted if he could compete with some of the dealers who came in regularly to complain about the price of everything and lament how bad business was. They were wide. He was sick of the restaurant, of dealing every day with food and with the public, but he was also sick of the street and the people who worked in it – including himself, maybe.

When he'd opened the place seven years ago, the street had been different. There had been a couple of second-hand clothes shops, a place that repaired violins, a record shop which specialized in obscure imports and sheet music. There had been a communal feeling. His had been the only restaurant, and the food had been thought of as unusual, even slightly exotic, at the time. Now it had become commonplace, and three other lunch places had opened up. The people he'd liked best had left: those who'd stayed had all had children and operations and tax bills and – business had become business.

But business was not good. He'd scarcely broken even on his first two years, and since then he'd become disenchanted with the work and had consoled himself by spending too much money – meals out with Nina, the woman he saw regularly but didn't live with, presents for her ten-year-old son, holidays abroad for the three of them – Greece, Turkey, Majorca. Over the last two years the tax man and the VAT people had started taking him seriously – examining his accounts closely, presenting him with outlandish bills and threatening to put him out of business. If he ever came through these tribulations, it would be as a slightly changed person, and he wasn't sure he liked the idea of the slight change. He'd been here too long. He wanted out, but for the moment there was no way out: he had to make the business pay to meet the outstanding bills.

The street, among those who had survived in it, had come to be called The Street.

He hurried down the stairs and greeted Paul, his back-up, who was waiting for him and reading a book. *Waiting for Godot.* Paul was a student of English Literature, making some money in the summer. He shut the book and pointed at the tray of morning rolls, telling him in detail how they'd been pissed on by a dog.

'So what else is new? Where's Lucy?'

'She'll be along.'

He glanced at Paul. Since he and Lucy lived together, they usually came to work together. Maybe something was up. Paul's thin face, with its sharp features, had set in an expression both hurt and spiteful.

Gus unlocked the door and they went in. He switched on the lights, the coffee machine, the hot water urn, the fan, the immersion heater. Paul started hacking apart a cabbage for the coleslaw.

Lucy came in, said sorry for being late and, without even acknowledging Paul, began peeling the beetroots she had remembered to boil yesterday afternoon. Something was definitely up. Lucy was a good worker, the best. She took care over the way she did everything, but at the same time she was efficient, fast. If there was no real work to do, she cleaned, dusted, put flowers in vases, polished mirrors, pictures, windows – she brought light into the place. If she and Paul split up, he might lose her.

He made the first flask of coffee and gave Lucy hers just the way she liked it, with the merest drop of hot milk, and was rewarded by her quick, frank smile. Maybe Paul was in a mood, maybe they'd had an argument, but she wasn't going to let it affect the way she was with others. If he'd been ten years younger and unattached, he could have gone for a girl like Lucy – or, maybe, she could have gone for him.

An American couple, tourists, all sweaters and slacks and moneybelts, came in wanting coffee and omelettes. Gus told them he wasn't open and didn't do omelettes. When they apologized cordially, he gave them the morning papers and told them he'd bring it to the table when it was ready. Paul gave him a dirty look over the shredded cabbage. There wasn't time to be making omelettes for tourists – there were too many other things to do. This was true, but what Paul didn't know was that he couldn't afford to turn away customers.

Lucy placed her first salad under the counter, behind the glass – beetroots, celery, orange, watercress, arranged in such a way that it looked beautifully simple, almost Japanese – and offered to beat the eggs for him. Paul rammed the carrots into the shredder and hunched his shoulders.

Gus was the restaurateur, he could do what he wanted, he was the owner. Big deal: he was also the cook, the maître-d' and the accountant. Nowadays he sometimes had to be the dish-washer and the floor-sweeper too. In a small place, you had to be too many people, you had to be all things to all men. Edinburgh was like that, a small place.

He should have settled somewhere else, but despite many long periods spent travelling in the seventies – India, Nepal, Sri Lanka, Thailand, Malaysia – and in the eighties – the States, Mexico, Peru – he had always been sucked back to Scotland, and more specifically, Edinburgh – as if some force were pulling him back. Nowadays everyone in Scotland was talking about Europe as if it had just been invented. It was like listening to kids thinking of opening their garden gate. He'd explored Europe so long ago that he could barely remember it.

He whisked the eggs and chopped some fresh basil he'd picked up by chance at the market yesterday. An omelette, properly cooked in the French way – maybe his experience of Europe had come in useful after all – was an art. Good food required both spontaneity and dedication. The simplest things could be the best. His own taste in food was like that: pasta with home-made pesto, green salad, good bread, a simple dry red wine.

When he thought about taking someone on, he always asked them to peel a potato. Some had done it before, others hadn't; some were neurotically fast, others mesmerizingly slow; some shredded the skin as they peeled it, others carved a careful spiral. It wasn't that he rated one way over another – he could just imagine working with somebody when he watched them peel a potato. Lucy had weighed the potato in her hand, looked at him and asked him what it was for, and when he'd told her he just wanted to see how she did it, she'd said that was a waste of a potato. He'd taken it out of her hand and asked her when she could start.

He made the omelettes and took them to the tourists, then their coffees. He hung around near their table for a minute, pretending to make small arrangements to a table nearby but in reality hoping for a compliment on the omelettes. When none came he went back to the kitchen area and started on the lunch dishes. You needed some feedback, some appreciation. When none came it was like being snubbed.

He had nightmares about sauces that burned, about those inspectors from the Department of Health who had invaded the kitchen without warning one day and examined his wooden spoons, his pots, his toilets. One of them had drawn his attention to the crumbs of food and grime trapped in a groove in the rubber seal of the fridge, and had ordered him to ventilate the toilets more adequately for their return visit the following week. There was a recurring one about the woman who had found a lump of jagged glass in her mayonnaise. The jar had broken, and he'd salvaged some of the mayonnaise. She had complained quietly, discreetly, when she could have taken him to court. He'd offered to pay for her lunch, which had only added insult to injury. No, she had made her point in the most polite way possible. She would not take it any further. She would not make a fuss. She would never eat here again, that was for sure, but she would not condemn him because of the lump of glass in her mouth. She was the kind of customer he could do with.

The compliment came when they ordered more coffee: the omelettes were *really* delicious, and they had never tasted parsley like that before – was it Scottish parsley?

When he'd laid out the trout in the oven dish and trailed the sauce over them, he put the dish aside and stopped for a coffee. He sat down at the staff table and leafed through a paper without reading it. The pizza and the quiche that hadn't sold yesterday were OK for today. The trout was prepared, so he needed two more hot dishes. He knew what they would be already: Aubergine Parmigiano, because he had the aubergines and had to cater for vegetarians, and Chicken with Mango, both of which he'd done the groundwork for yesterday afternoon. The aubergines were salted, washed, sautéed and presently congealing in a box in the fridge. The chicken had been roasted and dissected into portions. All he had to do was the sauces.

He had to keep getting up to serve people from the street who needed coffee before they opened up their own shops. Then he made the sauces, got all the hot dishes ready in time for lunchtime, but today there was no lunchtime rush. That happened sometimes. When everything was ready and waiting, twelve o'clock came and went and no one came, then one o'clock. Maybe it was the unusually hot weather. The weather, good or bad, was never good for business. The few regulars who trickled in today – they got on his nerves, but he needed them – didn't want his hot dishes but asked for finicky combinations of half-portions of salad. He told Paul off for cutting the tomatoes too thick for the tomato salad and for not using the basil.

By two o'clock no one was speaking to each other and the trout were already destined to become a cold trout mousse for tomorrow. He sent Lucy out for the cream cheese and told her to take her time and enjoy the sunshine.

He sat at the staff table drinking coffee, reading the papers and staring out the barred window. Since the restaurant was a basement, the only view was of the street literally at street level. He watched people's feet going by. Eventually he saw a girl's legs go by he wanted to go to bed with. Then the legs came down the stairs and he realized whose they were. She was too conscientious to linger in the sun and was already unwrapping the cream cheese and starting on the mousse. She was one of those people who would rather be doing something than nothing. Salt of the earth, but he wished she was happy.

It was three in the afternoon and the place was empty when Gus recognized the shoes of the down-and-out: they were heavy, shapeless, battered and soft, as if his feet were wrapped in layers and layers of soiled bandages. The man's steps had a slow inevitability about them, never really leaving the ground. His feet came down the stairs the way a child's would – both resting on each stair before going on to the next.

Had it taken him all day to raise the price of his pot of tea?

Gus lit another cigarette and pretended to engross himself in the crossword so that Paul would have to serve him. He didn't look up as the man shuffled past him but he could hear his laboured breathing, like the sound of coals shifting in a fire, the clatter of the tray as he hoisted it from the tray-rack, the crash of his assorted coins on the counter. Then the disarming politeness as he spoke, as if a dishevelled devil disguised a slick, well-mannered angel:

'Pot of tea for one, please.'

He was aware of the swathed bulk of the man swaying in and out of his field of vision as he tried to concentrate on the crossword. Paul, who still hadn't made it up with Lucy and was having a bad day, served him with pointed reluctance, barely concealing his resentment: he banged the teapot down on the tray, smashed his money into the till-drawer and turned away.

'Excuse me.'

Gus looked up, thinking the down-and-out was talking to him, but he wasn't: he was trying to get Paul's attention.

'Excuse me.'

Gus was about to intervene when Paul turned round and eyed the down-and-out with distrust.

'Are no strainers available?'

Gus almost laughed aloud. You had to admire the man's audacity.

'No.'

The man was about to take his tray and go, but suddenly Gus found himself on his feet. It was a policy in the restaurant to give every customer a tea-strainer with their pot of tea. It was meant to be one of the small, personal touches which might distinguish the place from others. These standards had to be maintained:

'Give the gentleman a strainer.'

Paul's eyes rounded with affront, then he sighed emphatically and turned away. He took his time about finding a tea-strainer, only to drop it with disgust on the tramp's tray.

'Thank you.'

He lumbered with his tray around the dividing wall and headed for his favourite seat in front of the mirror. He was their only customer.

What did he think about when he sat there in front of the mirror? Was he horrified by the sight of himself, of what he'd become? Or did he admire himself as a man who'd broken free of everything, even his own life?

Paul sat down opposite him with a belated lunch – the only portion of the Aubergine Parmigiano which would be eaten – and a glass of white wine. He opened his book and read as he ate, shovelling the food into his mouth without looking at it. That was what happened to most of the food you made – people ate it without noticing it.

'"People are bloody ignorant apes".'

Paul looked up from his book with a narrowed eye as he crammed another forkful of the Parmigiano into his mouth.

'It's a quote from that.'

He nodded at the book in Paul's hand.

Paul raised his eyebrows briefly. He seemed to think he was

the only person who read, and was never quite convinced when he mentioned a book.

'Have you read *Mercier et Camier*, the novel Beckett based it on?'

Paul shook his head and tilted his glass of wine this way and that.

'You should.'

But the student wouldn't be drawn. When he'd finished eating, he put the open book face down on the table and asked him for a light. As Paul took the lighter and lit up, he gave a backward nod of his head towards the corner where the down-and-out sat and said:

'That guy has to go, Gus.'

'Why?'

'He smells. He's scaring off the other customers.'

'What other customers?'

'Exactly.'

'He isn't the reason they're not coming in. It's a heatwave out there. We need to put some unusual cold drinks on the menu. Edinburgh tap-water, with ice and lemon.'

Paul wasn't in the mood for humour:

'That guy is bad news, Gus, and you know it.'

'So are a lot of our regulars.'

'You know what I mean, Gus. He's the kiss of death. If you don't want to tell him, I will.'

'If anyone tells him, I will.'

'You're the boss.'

Paul flicked his ash into the ashtray, though it didn't need to be flicked, and smoked his cigarette intensely. When it was half-smoked, he stubbed it out fussily, shut his book and took his plate into the kitchen area, where he stood with arms folded and glared at the door, as if defying anyone to come in. It was hard when there was no custom. It was hard for everyone.

Gus thought: '*Godot* doesn't seem to be teaching him much in the way of compassion for down-at-heel wayfarers.' Yet in a way the student was right.

He thought of a woman, he didn't know her name but she was a good customer – regular, appreciative, well-heeled – who often came in with her teenage kids. Their enthusiasm for the lemon cheesecake was heartening. She paid him the compliment of ordering one to serve at a dinner party. More than once she'd hinted that she'd like to run a restaurant herself. She probably imagined it as an extended dinner party. It didn't occur to her that the lemon cheesecake had become a daily chore for him, a meaningless ritual – he could no longer bear to taste it. But he'd concealed his nausea at the thought of making an extra one and had agreed to do it. The last time she had come in, now that he thought about it, was on one of the down-and-out's first visits, and she'd encountered him at the counter. He'd bumped into her with his tray. The tea-pot had overturned, and some tea had splashed on her arm. The tramp had apologized, then grinned and said:

'I'm glad that wasn't me!'

She'd eyed him with something like awe and replied that it was nothing.

She had behaved well, as one should, but she hadn't been back since.

Something had to be done about the down-and-out.

He found a recipe for Aubergine Pie which he could apply to the Parmigiano – all he really needed to add was some fresh basil, which he had. While he was rolling out the pastry, Paul chopped the basil and put it to him:

'He's been sitting there for an hour, Gus. The guy's asleep. Somebody should go over, clear his table.'

He didn't want Paul to do it – he would do it with such bad grace – but he didn't want to do it himself. He asked Lucy. She was cleaning the glass of the salad counter, but she didn't mind.

Paul looked at him with disgust.

He finished rolling out the pastry, laid it in the oven dish and started trimming it with scissors.

The scream was clean and startling – it sounded almost wholesome. They ran into the restaurant area, he clutching his rolling pin, Paul the knife he was using. They met Lucy rushing the other way, her hands covering her ears as if to block out the sound of her own scream.

He walked over to the table in the corner. The man had become a slouched statue of himself. He had not poured his tea. Gus put a hand on his shoulder and turned him a little. The grin had soured into a grimace, the green eyes had locked in their askew stares.

He turned to Paul, whose eyes were wider than he had ever seen them.

'An ambulance? You want me to call an ambulance? What's wrong with the guy, Gus?'

'Nothing's wrong with him. He's dead.'

Lucy screamed again. He told Paul to take care of her – it sounded like he was telling him to take care of her all the time, not just at this moment – while he made the call and locked the door.

He didn't want to leave the dead man. He sat down on a chair next to him and held his hand. It felt stiff and calloused, like the broad claw of a crab. He did not say anything. He was vaguely aware of people being turned away at the door, of Paul buzzing around, keeping people out and gesticulating at Lucy, who was now at the staff-table, her head in her hands. He closed his eyes and waited for the ambulance to arrive.

*

He poured some brandy into an empty tumbler and took it back to the table in the corner. He sat down and looked at himself in the wall-mirror: worried, tense, unhealthy. He thought of the corpses he had seen – in India, in Sri Lanka, in Peru. And the deaths he had lived through here in Scotland: his father floundering in his bed, gasping like a landed fish, a look of strained incomprehension on his face. His mother's slow, inexorable death, the erosion of her body and then her mind, until she believed that her bedside locker in the hospice was bugged. By comparison, the death of the down-and-out seemed serene, as if he had chosen it. And he knew this had been his first real death – the first death he felt truly involved in.

The others in the street would be waiting for him in Dr Jekyll's, the pub on the corner, waiting for the story of how the down-and-out had died. There was so little to tell, really, but already, in his mind, he was rehearsing how he'd relate the event – and in the pub, the other dealers would all chip in with their anecdotes about the down-and-out – maybe he'd find out who had given him the cigar – all relieved as hell that he was gone, then they'd close in on him to ferret out and relish every detail of the death, as if it concerned them. And maybe it did concern them, all of them. 'I'm glad that wasn't me!' – already he could hear himself quoting the down-and-out to the others, and they would smile, nod their heads, narrow their eyes and agree.

He stood up, cleared away his glass and his ashtray, switched everything off, put on his jacket, made to set the alarm, then he realized he hadn't swept the floor.

Me is the Problem

I wish above all to write of Beauty, but I have no experience of Beauty. I do not know how to write the beautiful English sentences, I have tried to speak them for so long, but they sound ugly in my mouth! It is more important that I tell the Truth. But I have no one to tell it, so I write it here, in this cash book from the restaurant.

For a great misfortune has befallen me. It happened last night on my way home. I am working all day in the restaurant, for I have been many years now a waiter. As regards who am I, I do not know. As regards which type waiter – you tell me. For I have been so many waiters, now I do not know which one to be.

Would you care to see the list, sir?

We have Indian, vindaloo or mild, baked in cream and fragrant spices or roasted on the tandoori. We have Chinese deep-fried in wok with chicken wings. We have Italians in black waistcoats and olive oil, French with raised sautéed eyebrow, or may I recommend a little Greek wrapped in vine leaves? British sir? I am afraid we are out of British waiters. We cannot get them fresh. Me, sir? You want *me*? Certainly, sir – and to follow, perhaps my family?

What will become of my family if it is found out? What will Perveen, my wife, say to me when the police shall come to my door and wish to interview me concerning this terrible event? It is destined – my description is printed in black and white in today's *Evening News* for all to see:

Police are anxious to interview a man in his forties of medium height and build, who was seen shortly after eleven o'clock last night near the scene of the murder. He has been described as balding, dark-skinned, dressed in a black suit and white shirt, and is thought to be of Indian, possibly Pakistani origin.

Every time I read this, I think – this could be anyone. Then I think – no, not anyone, but any one of us. Then I think – this could be no one except me!

It is four o'clock. Soon I will wash, I will shave, I will put on the clean shirt and I will catch a bus to the restaurant. Perveen has taken the children to her cousin's. I have an hour to do nothing. Any other day, this I would enjoy, this hour to be with myself, but today is not any other day. Today I am feeling like the actor before he goes to the theatre. I am nervous. I shall look over the menu as usual, but tonight it will be different, tonight it will be like the nervous actor going over his lines. Tonight I do not wish to be seen. Tonight I will envy the cook, the dishwasher. I like very much to hide in the kitchen with them.

Oh, I feel like this before. I am not suited to this work, this is true. I am not suited. The problem is I am myself also, I am me. Me is the problem. Like the little statue of a Scottish piper Perveen bought when we come to this country. It sits on the shelf above our bed. It is a heavy thing and we use it for a book-end. And Perveen, she uses it for a peg to hang up her necklaces. So, it is a book-end and it is a necklace-peg, but it is also a piper. I am a waiter and I am a husband and I am a father and I am a Pakistani, but I am also *me*.

Last night it is a Monday night and business is slow, so my uncle tells me I can get away early. It is wonderful. It is a warm night for this cold city of Edinburgh, people are walking in the streets without their woollen jerseys. There is, what is the word, the *illusion* of summer. So, I decide – why not take the long way home through the park? I have been buried in the restaurant the whole day, sweating like a pig in my tuxedo. I smell like a biryani, some fresh air will do *me* good. (You see? If it hadn't been for that *me* I would not be in this very sticky predicament I am landed in.) And I believe I shall have one pint of beer in the International Bar, for although it is not a nice place, the nice thing about it is that it is open late, and the people they know me there. They do not really know *me*, but they know my face. I am a regular.

So I walk through the park. I am looking forward to my pint of lager in the pub, I am thinking about the white froth on the top, the cold weight of the glass in my hand, the taste of it upon my tongue. So I am walking along between the trees and thinking what a wonderful land this is and one day my son Ahmed may grow up to be a great man here. Yes, with his good education he will flourish. I hope only that he does not have a restaurant, for I have seen what it has done to my uncle. He is all the time work, work, work. After the restaurant, the accounts, after the accounts, tomorrow's orders, after tomorrow's orders, tomorrow's menu. My uncle gave up his *me* a long time ago. I would rather that Ahmed learns how to write of Beauty, write the beautiful English sentences.

I am thinking these thoughts when I see, by the side of the path, a shoe.

This is not strange, for I have seen many shoes thrown away in parks before – where do they come from, who throws them away? – but this shoe is a shining black, patent-leather thing, high-heeled, and with a sort of bow at the front which is I think a kind of ribbon. It looks to me a very splendid shoe indeed.

I pick it up, I look at it. There is nothing wrong with it, it is perfect. I think to myself that Perveen would like very much a pair of shoes like this. I hold it this way and that, I am trying to see in my mind Perveen's foot in the shoe and yes, I believe the foot will fit. So I look about on the grass beside the path for the other shoe. If I find it, I think, I will take the pair home to let Perveen try them on for size. I do not find the other shoe however, so I walk along a little way with this one shoe in my hand, then I throw it away – what is the use of one shoe, even if it is good? I hurry on to the International Bar.

Then I see the other shoe. It is shining in the shadows under the bushes, but when I bend down to look, I see it has a foot in it. I find the leg of a woman. It is sticking out from under the bushes in a strange and difficult position. I see the body of the woman there under the bush. I hear a blast of music in my head – a chord, yes that is the word, a chord from the music in a movie is booming in my head. I am in a movie, I think, but of course I am not.

I can tell at once she is attacked, but I hope she is not dead. So I come down to take a closer look at her. Maybe she is drunk, for I know how some of these Scottish women drink. But when I lean over her I slip and fall against her. My hand touches her hair. Her head turns over. I see her white face and the dark blood at her mouth.

I don't know how I get out of there. I am walking very fast, then I am running. I want to shout to the people I see at the other side of the park walking their dogs, but I do not. I am more concerned with the sticky blood on my hand and my wrist. There is a smear of it on the sleeve of my white shirt.

I leave the path. I run across the grass. I see the swings and the climbing frame and the slide where I take Ahmed to play on days off. Everything is the same but everything looks different. The slide in the moonlight is like the curved blade of a knife. The chains of the swings look evil and the climbing frame looks like a device of torture.

I am dizzy, I feel sick. I stop to put on my jacket – I must at all costs hide the blood on my sleeve. A man comes towards me walking his dog. He looks at me. I know I should tell him but he turns away. I do not follow after him. Another man, he is jogging in his jogging suit. I almost say to him to stop, but he does not see me, he jogs past me behind the trees.

I am so thirsty, I need to have a pint of beer and think about what has befallen. I walk and walk. I am turning the corner into the street where we live. I am under the streetlamp outside my own house. I catch my breath. My heart is beating fast. I must decide what to do, I know this, but all I am thinking of is the blood on my shirt and the dead woman lying under the bush in the park. I try to clean the blood from my sleeve with my handkerchief, but my fingers are sticky with it. I throw the handkerchief into the litter bin. I walk past my own door, for I am not ready to go in. The light is on, I can see it above the curtains. Perveen will be there awake and she will see the state I am in and she will ask about the blood.

It is now that a man and his wife pass me by, but as they pass the man stops and he says to me: 'Is everything all right?' I nod my head, yes yes, of course, everything is all right, it is a beautiful warm summer night, everything is beautiful in your country. I am saying these things and I do not know what else I am saying. They move on along the street. Of course, they know me – they are my neighbours! And here I am leaning on my own fence outside my own house and I am laughing, because it is the first time they ever speak a word to me, these friendly neighbours – and when they do, what do they say? Is everything all right? And this is very funny indeed, for ever since I come to your country, I am all the time asking you if everything is all right, sir. Tonight I will say it again, over and over again, 'Is everything all right, sir?' I will say, but everything is not all right. Tonight, everything is all wrong, sir. With me, sir, me is the problem.

I know I should go to the police and tell them. I have done nothing, I am innocent – what have I to be afraid for? This is the reasonable thing to do, but do not ask me to be reasonable. Reasonable is finished, it is not now on the menu.

Now I look into the mirror and I see how I go sour. I curse myself as I am cursed – with the curse of the exile. Look at my skin, sir, at the brown skin. Take a good look, madam, see how brown I am. To you I am charred, I am a beast roasted in the ovens of hell. And – what is it you say? – as ugly as sin. See how the head grows bald, how the teeth go brown, how the skin creases like leather. Look into the eyes, sir, not at the yellow whites with the blood in them but the eyes, the black, black eyes.

Now, is everything all right, sir? Tell me, I need to know. Every night I am changing into my waiter clothes and I am making my bow-tie straight in the mirror and I am thinking: this cannot continue. It does, however. It is a spell upon me I cannot break. It is the one thing I can do in your country. So I am getting myself ready. Yes sir, certainly sir! Thank you, madam!

Where I am from, you ask? I ask you why you ask. This is of no importance. To speak of my past, it would be to tell you a dream. You would not understand the dream, madam, and I would change it to tell it in your words. Everything is so cold in your country, even your words are cold. My ears ache with them, my head is frozen. My heart it grows icicles. I forget my past like the dream it is. A bad dream, sir, a dream I do not wish to remember.

I do not wish to remember the present situation either. I mean last night, but I must. I must tell everything. At last, I come into the International Bar. I am a regular here. But this night, when I open the door, everyone looks at me! I walk to the bar. I order my pint of lager. It is when I lift the glass up to my mouth that I see how my hand shakes. I pretend to be watching the television above the bar. Soon I stop shaking enough to drink the beer. I order another, then I go to the toilet.

In the broken mirror I look at myself and I think, I am not the murderer, I am not the murderer. I wash my hands, I wash them very clean. I go back to the bar and I drink my second pint. I order another. I drink and I drink and I play the one-armed bandit. It is winning as usual. I am thinking to myself, at all costs I must behave as usual. I do behave as usual, but I drink more. I stay till the bar is closing. Then I walk home.

The house is dark, Perveen is I think asleep in bed. I go to the bathroom and I take off my shirt. I wash it until the blood is out of it. Perveen wakes up and comes through and she knocks on the door. She wants to know what it is I am doing in there at this time of the night. I am washing my shirt, I say, for it has a bad curry-stain. Give it to me, she says, but by this time the shirt is washed, there is no trace of the stain. I hang it up to dry and go to bed. I can't sleep. I worry about the people who see me in the park, about the handkerchief I throw into the litter bin, about the shoe – my fingerprints on the shoe! At last the birds are singing, it is getting light outside, and I sleep a little bit.

Today I buy the *News* and I read my description.

It is time. I will take the *News* with me. I do not wish to leave it here. If Perveen reads it, won't she know me? Someone may show it to her. Everyone will hear of this terrible thing which has befallen our community. *Thought to be of Indian, possibly Pakistani origin.* Although it is me, it is all of us. We shall all of us suffer for it – and I am to blame, me is the problem! Perhaps I go to the police tomorrow. Perhaps they will believe me – perhaps!

It is time.

Now, sir, madam. Allow me to take your coats, pull out your chairs. Take a seat. The waiter I am is up to you. If you wish, sir, certainly sir, I know exactly the waiter you mean. The waiter who will bow and will scrape and pay you too much of his time. I am like the bad actor who forgets his lines but must go on and play his part. Listen to the way I speak – what a mess I make of everything I say! I even try to speak in sentences, in beautiful English sentences! And the way I look at you, with big eyes like the puppy from the dog home! Why not you take me home with you? I say. I am new to this wonderful country. No sir, I do not know what is in the sauce, for the menu is a poem I learn by heart. I do not understand the poem, however. I eat what they give me in the kitchen, standing up with a plate in my hand. I will bow and scrape in and out of your meal the whole evening, sir, and look at your lovely charming wife with big orphan eyes. When there is nothing to do, I will do it for all to see. Rattle your bottle in your ice-bucket and you will see me run! Take out your cigarettes – I am here at your elbow with the lighter! Here I am, sir, at your service! Madam, may I refill your glass? Sir, may I compliment your wife on her choice of dress – and the shoes, such beautiful shoes!

Say Something

Wait for me Pete, will you, *wait*. Stop running away, will you, *wait*! Look, Pete, it's a doll. Somebody's gone and lost their dolly, Pete. *Pete*. Look, it's one of those dolls that can talk, Pete, I used to have one exactly like this. You pull the cord, see, like this ... Hear what she says, Pete? She says she's thirsty, Mummy. I'm thirsty too, Pete. Hear what she says, Pete? She says she wants a dwinkie. I wanna *dwinkie* too, Pete. A *big dwinkie*, Daddy! *I wanna gweat big dwinkie!* I want ... I want to sit down, Pete. I've got to ... sit down. Just for a minute. I'm sorry, I'm really, really sorry but ... I've just got to sit down for a minute. I just want ... one cigarette, Pete, then I'll come upstairs, OK? OK, Pete?

Shit. Oh fuck. Look at that. I've gone and dropped my make-up things all over the stairs!

Say something, will you, don't just stand there. *Pete!* You don't care, do you? You don't. I've dropped my make-up things all over the stairs. Somebody's gone and lost their dolly. A little girl's gone and lost her dolly, but you don't care. Do you, Pete? No, you don't care. You just stand there. You just stand there looking like ... like *you*. There's nothing else like it. You. You in a huff. You in a black, black mood. Oh say *something*, will you, for Pete's sake!

For *Pete's* sake! That's a good one!

She's laughing too, Pete! Did you hear her? She thought it was funny, didn't you dolly? It made you laugh, eh dolly? *Yes.*

Funny Mummy. But it didn't make Daddy laugh, did it dolly?
No. Because nothing makes old huffy Daddy laugh tonight,
does it? *No.* Cause old Daddy-waddy's gone into a gweat big
huffy-wuffy, hasn't he? *Yes.* Shall I tell you why, baby? He's
gone into a gweat big huffy-wuffy cause funny Mummy went
and got boozy-woozy at Daddy's little de-part-mental party!
Naughty Mummy! And now old huffy-Daddy isn't going to
speak to her for *days!* Is he, baby? *No!* Isn't that a terrible
thing, baby? It is. It is a terrible thing, isn't it? Not to speak to
somebody for days. Isn't it, Pete? *Pete?*

Please, Pete, say something, anything. Tell me I'm drunk as
a skunk. All right, I'm drunk as a skunk. I know I'm drunk as
a skunk. So what? Am I not s'posed to get drunk any more,
hmm? Am I not s'posed to enjoy the party? That's what
parties are for, isn't it Pete? For enjoying getting drunk as a
skunk. You said so yourself, Pete, you know you did. You said
just enjoy it, just be yourself. You said just enjoy the party
Isabel, just be yourself *Isabel.* You called me Isabel, you know
you did. That's why I got drunk. I was nervous, Pete. I'm
sorry, I'm really . . . really sorry. Oh, shit. Oh, fuck. I couldn't
help it. I got nervous cause you called me Isabel. You did.
Instead of Izzy like you usually do. So I knew you didn't really
mean enjoy the party, you didn't really mean be yourself. You
meant don't you dare do any such thing. You meant behave
yourself *or else.*

Or else *what?*

You meant be decorative, that's what you meant. Be the
New Blood's dec'rative fiancée! Be my formal little fiancée,
wear the frilly, floral thing I bought you for that purpose! Yes!
Act like a wifeling, be the New Blood's pretty wife-to-be! If
she's lucky! If she behaves herself! As long as she doesn't get
drunk as a skunk at the departmental party, eh Pete? As long
as she doesn't go and do something really inconsiderate, like

get herself pregnant again, for instance! Oh, that would really be the end, wouldn't it Pete?

That's what you meant, you know you did. You meant speak when you're spoken to, otherwise keep your mouth shut. You meant don't be yourself. For christsake, don't be *Izzy*! Not tonight! Not at the departmental party! Don't be natural, don't be relaxed! Not with the professor, at all costs! For godsake, don't say what you *think*! Don't disagree with the professor! Not about *literature*! Heaven forbid! Not about the role ... the *portrayal* of women – that's the word, isn't it, portrayal? – of women in Victorian fiction. Oh no. That's the professor's speciality. Women in Victorian fiction. Women in bloomers, in stays! He's an expert on bloomers and stays! That's his baby! Don't shoot your mouth off about the suffragettes, he's much too learned to disagree with! Learned! Old letch. His eyes were all over me, you *fool*! And the others, the others were worse. Your so-called colleagues, Pete. And that young one with the little beard he was trying to grow, the little pubic beard – what was he called again? You know the one I mean, Pete, the one wearing the jeans. The one with the cock in his jeans and the little pubic beard, the one you thought I fancied, Pete – who was he, and how come you've never mentioned him before? No you don't have to tell me, Pete, I remember. His name was Mike. He told me, he introduced himself over the vol-au-vents. He must be about the same age as you, Pete. Or is he younger? Another of the new bloods, eh? Is that where you got the idea of growing a beard, Pete? So that you and Mike could scratch your pubic beards together in the staff club over a couple of mature malts?

I don't like you with a beard, Pete. I know I said it suited you, but that doesn't mean I like it, right? Oh, it suits you. It suits you too much, just like the pipe. And I mean, you have to look older than the students to have some authority over them, eh Pete? Maybe you should get a walking stick, that would do the trick, wouldn't it, Pete? A knobbly old walking stick, and you could use it like the pipe, Pete, use it to point to things. Things like students. I mean, you've only had the job for a month, it's a one-year contract, but already you look like you're in with the bricks. That jacket, Pete, that tweed jacket. I never thought I would live with a man who wore a tweed jacket. You are really boring, Pete, you know that? I feel sorry for myself, I really do.

Come on, Pete, you can tell me about Mike – is he a friend or an enemy? A rival? You should watch him, Pete, he's got horrible little close-set eyes like a ferret. What he was doing to me with his ferrety little eyes. And the wives, did you notice the wives, Pete? Christ, Pete, you don't really want me to look like one of them, do you? The professor's wife – did you see what she was wearing, Pete? She was wearing the fucking curtains, Pete! And the shoes – Jesus, Pete, who the fuck did she think she was – Shirley Temple on acid? And the others, did you look at them, at what they were wearing, Pete? Have you ever seen so many cardigans in one room? Like a fucking cardigan convention, if you ask me. I looked at them, Pete, and they looked at me. Oh yes, they incinerated me with their eyes. That's a good word, eh Pete? Incinerated? I know where I learnt that word, Pete.

Say something, Pete. Please say something.

I'm not s'posed to say a word. I'm not s'posed to get drunk. I'm not s'posed to try, to *try* to *enjoy* . . . Admit it, that's what you meant, isn't it Pete? You meant don't dare enjoy the departmental party, or else. Or else I'd pay for it. All right, I'm paying for it now. And I'll go on paying for it for days. Won't I, Pete? *Pete?*

You meant be Isabel. Be a good little dolly. I tried, Pete, I really did, but I s'pose I'm just Izzy, I'm fed up trying to be Isabel, so there. Put that in your PhD and smoke it.

Somebody's gone and lost their dolly. Look at her, Pete. Isn't she pretty? And she can talk. Listen.

She says she's hungry, Mummy! I'm hungry too, Pete. Seriously, Pete, I was expecting something real to eat, not a cube of cheese and a chipolata impaled on a fucking toothpick. And the vol-au-vents, I still don't know what was in those vol-au-vents, but it tasted like cold tapioca, like wallpaper paste. Ugh! I'm ravenous, Pete, I've never been as hungry in my life. Come over here and I'll show you how hungry I am. No? What is it, are you scared I'll bite?

Say *something*. Go on, tell me I'm a drunken slut. Tell me how terrible I've been. How mortified you were when I dropped my wine. All over the white linen tablecloth, all over my new flowery dress, all over the stinking rotten carpet. I spoiled it all, didn't I Pete? The tablecloth, the dress, the carpet . . . Your chances of a ruined new . . . I mean a *renewed* contract. Ruined your career, didn't I Pete? Just because I spilled a little wine, a little red wine. A little red wine isn't so bad, is it, Pete? It isn't as bad as blood, not as bad as spilling blood, new blood. You're the New Blood lecturer, aren't you? So you should know. Tell me then, I need to know. Really I do . . . I really do need to know, Pete. It's worse, isn't it, to spill new blood?

Get your old ethics textbook out and tell me.

OK, don't. Don't say anything at all. Just stand there. Just stand there looking like you.

Your glasses are steaming up again, Pete.

I wonder why they do that. You know what, Pete, why is it that no one ever invented windshield-wipers for glasses? I mean, when your glasses got wet tonight, I mean when I threw that glass of wine over you, that other glass of wine somebody gave me to replace the one I'd spilled all over your career, well, remember how it went all over your glasses? Well Pete, now think about this. If you'd had a little button in your pocket you could've pressed to activate the wipers, maybe it wouldn't have been so bad for you, eh Pete? You men like pushing buttons, I've noticed that. You've pushed my button, Pete, and now it's time to drop the bomb. The only kind of bomb we women ever drop, Pete.

I'm really sorry for throwing the wine at you, Pete, but it was the way you were talking to me, through clenched teeth like that, the way you were gripping my arm and leading me out of the room . . . You were hurting me, Pete. At least no one saw me do that, eh? Isn't that something to be thankful for? At least you'd got me out of the room before I threw the wine at you. It would've been worse if you'd been wearing your contacts. How are your contacts, Pete?

Oh, yes, I forgot. I'm sorry I stood on one of your contacts, Pete. But that's what happens in the academic business, isn't it? You end up with a fiancée who stands on your contacts.

Do your contacts get steamed up the way your glasses do? No, really, Pete, I'm curious, I'm interested to know. I remember being with you somewhere, Pete. Either the botanical gardens or a cafe with a lot of pot plants. Anyway, when we went in, your glasses steamed up. And I looked at you Pete, and you know what you looked like? You looked like a Dalek, Pete. A steamed-up academic Dalek. If you think I'm going to spend the rest of my life with a steamed-up academic Dalek like you, you've got another think coming.

You've always got another think coming. That's what you're paid to do. You're paid to think, Pete, and you know it! But you don't think, you don't really think at all. You mouth your footnotes like flea-bitten animals grunting at each other in the zoo. That professor of yours looks exactly like a yak, don't you think?

Why are you gripping the banister like that? Hmm? Your

knuckles've gone all white. You've gone white all over, Pete. What d'you think you're doing, palely loitering? Palely loitering. It's unhealthy. You've been taking too many of those tutorials. You look like a ghost. Worse, you're as white as a thesis. An unwritten one, one that just can't seem to get written. That one you kept telling me about the first time I got pregnant, that one you had to get finished then! That one you still have to finish! *Then* we'll move out of this dump. Then we'll get a bigger flat, have a baby! Not yet though, oh no! You just stand there looking like a silent seminar, like the ghost of an unwritten thesis, looking down at me like—

All right, go ahead and look! This is me, Pete, this is who I am!

At least I can still do that, Pete. I can still look at myself. Can you do that, eh? What do you think you see when you look in the mirror, Pete? Apart from a bit of designer pubic beard and a thorough understanding of your period?

I have a thorough understanding of my period as well. Don't you think I wanted it to come? Don't you think I've been praying for it to arrive?

You don't know what it was like for me to grow up. At the school I went to, I was expelled. That's what happened to me, Pete. I got fucking well expelled. All right, I know you know about that, I know I've told you about that before, but I haven't told you why, not really. You know why I got expelled, Pete? I want to tell you this, I have to tell somebody this so I suppose it'll have to be you. I got expelled because . . . They had this school council, a kind of mini-parliament, except we were all girls of course because it was a girls' school – can you follow that, Pete? Just stop me if there's anything you don't understand – and so anyway, I was expelled because I brought up the subject of our periods at the school council. Seriously. You know what we had to do? If a girl was caught unawares by her period, which happened all the time, because girls of that age aren't always all that regular as I'm sure you'll remember if you think hard, Pete. But I'm forgetting – you don't think, do you, Pete? Oh well, just let me think for you and give your brain a rest. Anyway, the girl in question had to go through this great rigmarole to get a sanitary towel, right? She had to request permission to leave the classroom, she had to go to the games teacher, who had the key to the cupboard, the cupboard where the sanitary towels were kept. I'm sorry if this is disgusting you, Pete, but it's true. The truth is disgusting sometimes, the truth is never pleasant, otherwise it wouldn't be the truth. I expect you've read a book or two about the truth, Pete, eh? Your kind of truth. Anyway, to get back to my kind of truth, this sanitary towel from the games mistress had to last you all fucking day. And the thing was, of course, everybody knew, when they saw you being led through the corridors by the games mistress to the cupboard, everybody *knew* . . . But that wasn't the worst of it, the worst of it was that when you'd finished with your sanitary towel, you had to put it in this disposal bag and *give it to the janitor*! Can you believe it, Pete? Can you understand what I'm telling you? That was why I was 'asked to leave' school. I raised the issue of the issue, and the disposal of, the sanitary towels with the school council.

Aren't you proud of me, Peter?

You fucking should be.

See? I called you Peter. I did. I called you Peter, Pete, so that's what you are to me now. Peter. All right, Peter, although I never thought I'd live with anybody called Peter, what about sex then, Peter? Isn't that what you want now? To atone for my sins at the departmental party in bed. And how.

Why don't you edit a volume on the subject, Peter? I could do your research for you, I could *be* your fucking research, *and* type out your boring footnotes, make the coffee, dress up as a schoolgirl-whore-nun who demands to be dominated. What d'you think? Isn't there a monogram in it somewhere? All right, Peter, come on, dominate me. I demand to be dominated. Come on, Pete, dominate me, all over. Really, it would make a fucking change!

No? Oh, so that's how it is, is it? No sex, please, we're English Literature. We'd rather interpret 'The Wife of Bath's Tale' again, in the original! Of course, we wouldn't touch a real Wife of Bath with a fucking barge-pole, oh no!

Don't look at me like that!

Don't. Please. I'm sorry. I'm really . . . really. You know I can't stand it when you look at me like that. Like I'm some kind of despicable . . . *thing*. I'm not a thing, I'm Izzy. Don't you understand? Don't you like Izzy? You used to say . . . You didn't look at me like a thing. Maybe that's what you want me to be, Pete, is that it? A plaything. And a work-thing. And a sex-thing. And a little wifeling-thing. I can't be all those fucking things! Not any more, Pete. That's what you want all your so-called colleagues to think, isn't it Pete? Oh here's the New Blood, with his *thing*! She's quite sexy, quite pretty, pretty good in the sack I imagine, I imagine she's quite the *thing*! Good for the New Blood, well done the New Blood!

This is what you really want, Pete. A doll. A doll called Isabel. Dress her up in a pretty floral thing. Take her to the departmental party. Then undress her again, take her to bed. That isn't all you want from me, is it Pete?

It's a pity she talks so much, isn't it Pete? Listen. She says she's sleepy, Mummy. I'm sleepy too, Pete. I'm so tired I could sleep for a hundred years, a hundred years, a hundred years. I could do that, Pete, but you wouldn't chop the trees down, would you? You wouldn't wake me with a kiss. No, because your kiss, with that little pubic beard of yours, would send me into a fucking coma!

OK, turn your fucking back on me, if you can't stand to look at me. Turn your back on everything, go on. Everything you can't deal with. It's yourself you can't deal with, not me.

A little girl's gone and lost her dolly, but you don't care, do you Pete?

I want you to care. Everyone has to care. I want to care for it. I don't want to lose it. Not this time, Pete. I want to keep it, to hold it, to care. I don't want to have to . . . You shouldn't make me have to . . . No one should be made to have to . . .

The Gargle

She woke up to the sound of her husband gargling in the bathroom. She listened to it for a moment, appalled, then closed her eyes and let out a sharp cry of disappointment: it was Friday, but she wasn't meeting Mike. She covered her head with the pillow, but Douglas's gargle was one of those noises that were impossible to ignore, like the medieval plumbing or the old couple upstairs making love. The man always sounded like a labouring tuba, the woman an out-of-tune clarinet. The bed and floorboards provided the rhythm section. The gargle was like that – once you were aware of it, you started listening for it even though it made you shudder.

Everything about Douglas had become irritating. The way he smiled, showing all his mean white teeth and bringing the crow's feet at the corners of his eyes into high relief. He'd been smiling like that for so long, the smile had become a mask. He wore the smiling mask almost all the time, but behind it the face was sour and vengeful. Mind you, the mask was scarier than the face. She wished he'd drop it and show her his true hatred, instead of trying to use sarcasm.

He hadn't been using sarcasm as much since she'd started having the affair with Mike. Maybe he suspected something. It wouldn't be the first time. Now they only spoke to each other when it was necessary, usually to discuss money. Bills that needed to be paid, the balance of the account – what he called the 'household account', the one she had access to because there was never anything in it. He had other accounts. Or sometimes it was the car or the children, but whatever it was, they would only discuss it when it had become a problem, a bone of contention. When they weren't arguing about something, they maintained a mutual, silent hostility. Sometimes he broke this unexpectedly. As soon as he'd come in the door from work, he'd put the smiling mask on and say something like: 'And how is my darling wife?' That was the sarcasm. Or sometimes, out of the blue, he would demand sex. It was like somebody demanding a refund for goods which had proved to be imperfect.

She had given up having headaches, backaches and fictional periods. Such excuses only made him all the more determined to have his way. It was easier to let him and get it over with as quickly as possible. Douglas sensed the futility of it too, but was unable to relinquish something he saw as his right. She couldn't believe that he actually enjoyed it – maybe there had been more of a challenge for him when she'd put up resistance.

She was living with a stranger. It was scary. Sometimes when he looked at her she had no idea what he was thinking or feeling. It wouldn't surprise her at all to discover that he was thinking of intricate ways to dispose of the corpse.

She lifted the pillow from her ear tentatively. He seemed to have stopped gargling. He must be shaving. Shaving and reshaving. His growth was so thick, he had to do it twice every morning. Even so, he had a permanent five o'clock shadow. His bodily hair, once a source of amused wonder, had recently started to bring her out in a rash. It reminded her of the pelt of some miserable, furtive animal that had to hunt for its food in a cold climate. The hair was black and made his pale body look all the more naked and vulnerable. It felt abrasive against her skin. He was hopelessly apologetic about the rashes, and about sex in general, after the event. His orgasms were convulsive, and left him collapsed on top of her and gasping for breath, in a state of distress. In the past she'd sometimes felt moved to ask him if he was all right. Now she didn't even do that. What bothered her most was the forlorn groan of loss he would sometimes utter as he came to his solitary climax. It was a terrible sound because of its loneliness. But it wasn't as bad as his gargle.

He was at it again. Why was it so unbearable? It was something to do with the way he managed to go through all five vowels, as if his innards were trying to speak to her. That was a weird idea. It made her feel ill just thinking about it. Sometimes her mind did this to her, forcing her to think about things that made her feel ill. Sometimes she imagined people without their skins, with all the muscles and tendons and arteries and nerves showing, like those horrible, coloured illustrations in Mike's medical text-books.

She wished she could go back to sleep, back to that dream. Mike had been so un-bastard-like in it, so unlike himself in fact. He'd been an angel to her. She'd been crying and he'd come to her and wrapped her in his arms and kissed her stinging cheeks, looking into her eyes with solicitous love . . . He'd never looked at her like that in real life, of course. If he had, would she have fancied him in the first place? That was not the attraction. For her the attraction was clear. It was about using and being used. Some of her friends disapproved, and even took Douglas's part. They didn't understand her need.

Mike understood that, if nothing else. It fitted his own requirements. He was so busy with his work, it was all he had time for really. It was what he wanted too: no strings, no commitments, no messy emotional entanglements. It was the first time she'd had it so zipless – and now she'd have to do without it!

*

She'd met him when she'd had a routine breast-cancer test. While he was probing her fatty tissues, she'd asked him calmly if he enjoyed his work. He'd muttered something about somebody having to do it. She'd embarrassed him, but there was a flicker of interest in his eyes. She'd flirted with him openly enough to let him know it was on if he wanted it, and had mentioned a film she was thinking of seeing at the Odeon. Had he seen it? No? Then he must. So she'd contrived the date with him. Since then she'd been meeting him every Friday afternoon, at his place, and at other irregular times when he wasn't working and she could get away. The lengths she had sometimes gone to to get away for a hurried half-hour with him! It was like a drug.

What had he been saying in the dream? Just as she was on the point of remembering, there it was again, the gargle. It sounded like somebody drowning. Or maybe it was more like laughter, an eerie kind of underwater laughter, how laughter would sound to somebody who was drowning . . . She imagined herself as the one who was drowning, and Douglas standing up on the bank – laughing! That was probably just what he'd do.

She pulled the pillow down and breathed in quickly, then heard what was unmistakably the sound of Douglas's urine rattling into the toilet bowl. She ducked under the pillow again. She had a sudden image of him standing in the bathroom, in front of the toilet bowl, dressed in a wet-suit, flippers and snorkel. It was comical, but it was perfectly in character. He was weird enough.

She wouldn't be surprised if he did drown in the bathroom one of these mornings. His ablutions were obsessive. The range of deodorants and conditioners and pre-shave lotions and aftershave lotions and hair-gels . . . squadrons of aerosols and roll-ons and jars and tubes. They queued up four-deep on the shelves and formed a kind of procession around the bathroom, invading every available surface, even the top of the cistern, even the corners of the bath. It was a phobia, and still he managed to leave the house every morning looking like a frayed doormat.

She heard the plug being pulled, the insistent dribbling of the cistern filling up again, and on top of that something else – the noise of the pipes. A high whining sound. A thin sort of scream, like the scream of a terrified rodent. Or one of Mike's opera records – that one that always got stuck when the soprano reached for her highest note. It had happened once at exactly the wrong moment. They'd both tried to ignore it, but after a few minutes of Madame Butterfly having her multiple orgasm, she'd given up on her own and requested Howlin Wolf. At least if he got stuck in his groove, she wouldn't notice.

It was time to get up, go down and make the breakfast, get the kids ready and out to school, think about the shopping and the laundry! And it was Friday, the day she should be looking forward to. She'd called him last night, as usual, to arrange it, but he'd said he needed some time on his own! Had he found somebody else? Of course he had! The way he'd spoken to her on the phone last night, as if he was explaining something to a child – and him ten years younger! She'd suspected it last Friday, from the way he'd touched her, as if his fingers were preoccupied with the memory of another body. Probably one of those young nurses. They could make their uniforms look sexy if they wanted to. Or a patient. Maybe he'd fallen for some helpless young Pre-Raphaelite-looking patient in a white nightie. If only she had some idea what the new woman was like, she could compete, outdo her at whatever it was he wanted from her. There was the fear, though, that it might be sex. Let it not be. Let him be deeply in love with her, let him be infatuated, let him respect her intellectually, let them have everything in common – she was willing to be surpassed in these respects if only there was no competition between the sheets!

With the pillow pressed hard against her ear, it was difficult to tell if it was Douglas gargling again or the sink being unplugged and the water gurgling down the drain, but whatever it was she couldn't escape it. It made her shudder, clench her fists and shut her eyes so tightly that two hot tears squeezed out between her eyelids. Even if she did more or less block the gargle out, it would go on in her imagination – as it would in any case once he'd finished. Sometimes it returned to haunt her at the oddest moments – in the middle of the day, when she was loading the tumble-drier. Or worse, on a Friday afternoon, when she was in bed with Mike, just at the critical moment: Mike would moan throatily and all she could hear was Douglas gargling in the bathroom. At such moments she'd cling to him desperately – if their position allowed her to; if not she'd flail around wildly to grasp some part of him, a knee or an elbow, anything – and she'd hold on tight and charge into the orgasm like a hunted animal running for cover.

It was ironical that on these occasions Mike always commented afterwards that it had been *really* good, while smoking a cigarette as reflectively as he could and lounging back on the pillows, one hand behind his head, for all the world like some ham-actor in a B-movie for kids, playing the recumbent and tyrannical emperor. The naïvety of his vanity touched her in a way she couldn't explain. He was a child, a spoiled child, used to getting what he wanted, but his selfishness amused her. The little drama of his own life was so important to him – and she, despite herself, found it irresistible! But not this afternoon – he wanted to be on his own! Of course it was the beginning of the end. She had always known it could never last. Now she would be returned to the life she'd lived before she'd met him, but with a deeper feeling of emptiness and the guilt growing inside her like a tumour. She'd be returned to the rumbling, screeching plumbing, to the old couple upstairs making their laborious love, to Douglas and his gargle!

He was doing it again, deliberately, to spite her! He must be! He must know it made her feel ill! She hid her head deeper under the pillow, but the gargle went on and on, until it was the ghost of the gargle, amplified and distorted in her memory, until she was drowning in his laughter, until his innards were crying out to her, pleading with her ... The gargle would never stop.

A Good Night's Sleep

Just when he was maybe beginning to fall asleep at last, George Lockhart, an insomniac, thought he heard something bumping softly against his door. He opened his eyes to the darkness and listened. There it was again, against the door of his flat, soft but insistent.

He tried to rearrange himself more comfortably in the bed and sighed a sleepless curse. The noise had been getting to him lately. All the noises from the street below. Lockhart lived on the third floor of a tenement building in Edinburgh and although the street he lived in wasn't one of the busiest, there were always these noises puncturing the quiet – squeals of taxi-brakes, car doors being slammed, the Muzak from the late-night bar downstairs. When the bar closed, a few of its customers usually stood around on the pavement outside, gabbling loudly. Once they'd said their repetitive goodnights, there was usually a lull and sometimes he managed to get to sleep before the Chinese restaurant closed up. The staff always seemed to be having a heated controversy as they set the alarm, locked up, ignited their engines and roared off to the casino. Often too there were bands of students being extrovert on the way home from their pubs and their parties, and more than once that inflated laughter had set him thinking about his own student days, the flats he'd lived in then, the parties he'd gone to, the girls he'd gone out with . . . set him thinking, and so kept him awake. Worse were the tribes of drunks, branding the night with their threats, their slogans and their chants. And then there were the miscellaneous voices of the night – the garbled, gruesome shouts of the forsaken and the damned.

Something bumping softly against his door.

Sometimes there were noises from the building itself as well as the noises from the street. The old guy with the limp who lived upstairs. He was always coming home wildly drunk, and Lockhart would have to listen to his demented monologue as he heaved himself up the stairs, stopping every few steps to argue with some remembered or imagined enemy. Worse were his bouts of song. Amplified and distorted by the stairwell, they sounded like the wails of a wounded, cornered animal. And of course there were the people through the wall, the new people who'd moved in recently and who were always having rows. They'd had one of their disputes tonight, complete with slamming doors and breaking glass. A strained silence, then the muted duet of argument that meant they were over the worst of it. After a while, he'd heard them going out. He was anxious to be unconscious before they came home and started kicking their shoes off, playing their blues records and making it up in bed – their good times could be just as noisy as their bad.

Now this, surely not the wind, in any case not worth paying any attention to.

It was urgent that he fall asleep immediately because, as well as an insomniac, Lockhart was a teacher of Communication and General Studies, with the first year first thing in the morning. He'd got them having a series of discussions recently on the Problems of Modern Society. They'd done Pollution. Unemployment. Race Relations. Last week it had been Drugs and tomorrow it was what?

He turned over and tried to concentrate on not thinking about anything, so that maybe he wouldn't and therefore go out like a light – as if sleep could be crept up on from behind and be taken unawares. Of course he knew, from the yawning years of wrestling with his demons, as the dawn light seeped through his curtains, that sleep couldn't be crept up on, couldn't be taken unawares. It had to take you – a bit like orgasm and, as far as Lockhart was concerned, nowadays every bit as longed for. It was months since he'd slept with anybody and now he didn't know which he needed most – the sleep, or the anybody.

He punched the pillow, clenched his teeth, rearranged his legs and his arms. It was one of those expensive beds, scientifically designed for the sleepless, but single when all is said and as such harder than some. He tried not to think of Elaine, his ex-wife, sleeping in their old, comfortable double bed – alone? – and tried not to start worrying about what to do with Ben, their son, when he took him for the weekend . . .

He heard it again then, against the door of his flat, softly bumping. It wasn't anyone knocking and anyway – why knock? There was a doorbell. And it was too soft to be the old guy with the limp staggering against the door on his way up to his own. This was a different kind of pressure on the door, ceasing and coming again, not making much noise maybe but enough to keep insomniacs awake. Surely it couldn't be the new people, locked in a passionate embrace against his door, unable to wait until they'd unlocked their own?

He propped himself up on one elbow, switched on the bedside lamp and gave the clock-without-a-tick a dirty look. The time it told wasn't the right time, because Lockhart had developed the habit of setting it ten minutes fast, so that if need be he could take ten minutes longer to surface in the morning – as if time could be stolen from Time. Even so it said 01.45 – the wrong time for a visitor. Maybe it could be that stray cat he'd invited in not so long ago for the remains of a Chinese carry-out – back for its banana fritter? If so, he'd wring its neck.

But no, there it was again, something leaning then not leaning on the door, something bigger than a cat, something heavier and by the sounds of it, less likely to go away.

Tying his dressing gown on, Lockhart stamped along the chilly hallway in his bare feet, switched on the light and unlocked the door.

'Yes?'

The young girl sitting on his doormat looked up sharply as she spat out this affronted 'Yes?', for all the world as if he'd just barged into her bedroom. Maybe he had. He apologized:

'I'm sorry, but I heard . . . I wondered what the . . .'

Lockhart held the door half-closed and moved from foot to foot in the icy draught, scarcely able to believe that she was there on his doormat, talking to him with such emphatic scorn.

'What are you doing . . . out here?'

'I was *trying* to sleep!'

'Out *here*?'

'What does it look like?'

He had to admit that it did. She had spread out an assortment of brightly coloured but tattered clothes on the landing and had bundled others up into what looked like a makeshift pillow.

He watched as she took a pair of lumpy woollen socks from a plastic carrier bag and tugged them on over her jeans, every so often glaring up at him suspiciously. He went on staring helplessly as she tied on her worn sneakers, taken aback by her presence – by those glowering dark eyes, by the delicate cheekbones and lips. She was young – in her early twenties, maybe younger.

'Don't you have anywhere to *live*?'

'I wouldn't be here if I did, would I?'

'No . . . I suppose not.'

'You suppose right. I'm homeless, that's all. I've been sleeping in stairs for long time now.'

'But . . . you're young!'

'So? A lot of young people are homeless nowadays – haven't you heard?'

The teacher of Communication and General Studies hopped around in the icy draught and had to admit that he hadn't.

'Well you have now. Goodnight. George.'

He was startled by her use of his name, then laughed nervously. Of course, it was on the door. She echoed his nervous laugh perfectly, then dropped it suddenly and averted her face.

'But surely there must be somewhere you can go – a hostel, maybe?'

'Which hostel is that?'

'A hostel, I don't know, for the homeless.'

'They don't let me in any more, so I sleep in stairs. Tragic, isn't it? If you know what *tragedy* is.'

Lockhart found himself thinking of a grey-haired king wandering around in the homeless wilderness of a first-year literature option, the Fool at his side, but the doorstep at two in the morning was no place for a tutorial.

'Are you a student?'

'What's it to you? You a teacher?'

Lockhart nodded. The girl stopped blowing into her hands to laugh derisively.

'I might've known it. You look like the sadistic type.'

Lockhart ignored this.

'Where were you living before?'

'Before what?'

'Before you weren't.'

'Listen, teacher, listen carefully. I had to leave the place I was in. Now I don't have anywhere else to go, so I'm homeless. Got it? Sleep well.'

'But that's terrible!'

'No it's not. I'll die, that's all. I'll die and I don't care anyway and don't start telling me you do because you fucking well don't, nobody does.'

She glared up at him as she spat out the words. Lockhart stood there holding the door and saying nothing. What was there to say to a young girl who was going to die on your doormat at two in the morning?

'You wouldn't have a *cigarette*? Oh, I don't suppose you *smoke* though, do you?'

Lockhart replied stiffly that he did smoke, told her to wait a minute, then let the door swing closed on her. He could lock it now, go back to bed, forget her, get a good night's sleep yet if he dropped off right away. After all – why should he have to bother with her? Why did he feel obliged to try and do something to alleviate her plight? Maybe it was the way she sneered as she spoke to him, as if he personally was somehow to blame for her situation.

Back in the warmth of his bedroom, Lockhart lit a cigarette for himself and donned his socks. He could offer her the boy's room for the night. What harm would it do? Or if she preferred, she could just get some rest on the couch until the morning. Or he could call the police. Wouldn't a cell be better than the cold stone landing of a tenement stair, with a doormat for your mattress?

He yawned his way back out to the door. As he stooped to give her the cigarette and the lighter, he noticed the frayed hole in her old pullover and thought he caught a whiff of something bad – like rancid butter, but worse. As she handed back the lighter she bared her teeth in the parody of a smile and said:

'Thank you *so much*. You're *so kind*.'

He wasn't used to being the target for such venom and didn't know how to react. He hovered over her in silence, holding the door with one hand and smoking with the other. She looked up at him once, laughed sarcastically and looked away. At length, he came out with it:

'OK. You can stay the night here. My son isn't here at the moment. You can take his bed.'

He was just about to add that it was only for one night, that he had to get up early for work and that he'd want to see her gone in the morning, when she interrupted:

'No way.'

'But I'm offering you a place to *sleep*!'

The word echoed in the hollow stairwell. She glared at him insolently, over her shoulder, her lips parted slightly as if ready to laugh at him at any moment. Then she flicked her ash on the doormat, looked away and shook her head.

'Come *on*! It's a bed for the night!'

'I've heard that one before!'

'Oh for christsake, I'm not going to . . . *do* anything!'

She glanced at him with blatant accusation, as if to say that because he'd mentioned it, he must have thought about it.

Lockhart groaned with emphasis and waited. He thought she might be hesitating, but it was taking too long and so he told her that he had to sleep, had to get up early and he hoped she'd find a place to stay soon.

As he turned the key in the lock he heard her, on the other side of the door, bid him a quiet goodnight, all hostility gone from her voice, without that sharp edge of scorn.

Lockhart thumped the light switch with the side of his fist and padded back along the hallway to bed. Turning over and over in the warmth of it, trying not to think about her out there on his doormat, he heard it again, the soft bumping sound as she leaned back against the door. She must be trying to get comfortable, or not comfortable exactly but into a position for sleep. Lockhart endeavoured to do the same. Then he heard her coughing, weakly at first, then it was a harsh, hacking cough that echoed in the stairwell. She was definitely going to die out there and she didn't care – *And don't start telling me you do because you fucking well don't. Nobody does!* – and Lockhart wondered if he'd maybe been too impatient with her. Yet he felt angry too, angry with her arrogance: how dare she not care about herself! Why should he care about her, if *she* didn't? Why should anyone?

Again he heard her cough.

When he could suffer it no longer, he climbed out of bed again and switched on the lamp. Then he heard the voices outside, in the stair. It was the couple next door, the new people. He couldn't make out what they were saying, but the man's voice was raised. His wife's voice was high-pitched, accusing. He thought he heard the young girl – her sneering rejoinder. After a few minutes the voices subsided. Then he heard the key rattling in the lock of the flat next door. He hurried out and unlocked his door in time to catch his neighbours closing theirs. The woman was already inside, but the man stopped on his threshold when he saw Lockhart. There was no sign of the young girl. Lockhart found himself apologizing again:

'Sorry. I heard the . . . I wondered what the . . .'

'Oh, it was just some junkie sleeping in the stair.'

'Really?'

'Yeah. I told her where to go.'

'Did you? Where?'

'Where d'you think?'

Lockhart glimpsed his neighbour's tight little smile before the man turned and stepped into his hallway.

'See you.'

'Yes, goodnight.'

They locked their respective doors.

Lockhart switched off the lamp, then stepped over to the window, parted the curtains and peered down into the dark canyon of the street. He couldn't see her anywhere, but her voice was still there in his head, bidding him a quiet goodnight as he locked the door on her, as if she'd felt able to own up to her helplessness only with the door between them.

He turned from the window but didn't get into bed. What was the hurry? The luminous digits on the clock told him in any case that he'd never get a good night's sleep now. He stood in the darkness of the room, listening to the woman through the wall kicking off her shoes one by one, to the voices resuming their duet, to the music with its thudding bass, the man's laughter and the woman's shrill cry of mock surprise ... Didn't they have work to go to in the morning, these new people? He had the first year, and another of the many Problems of Modern Society. It had to be homelessness.

He climbed into bed, closed his eyes and immediately began to drift into a deep, deep sleep, then he heard it again, against the door of his flat, soft but insistent.

The Long Way Home

George Lockhart, the teacher who was still learning, lingered in his cramped classroom long after the night-class had shambled out of it, tacking things up on the walls.

The class had been the first unit in a module he'd put together on the History of the Working Classes – and it hadn't worked. Even his 'Day in the Life of a Coal-heaver', which he'd enjoyed making up, had sounded trite and unconvincing in his mouth. Towards the end of the session a faint-hearted feminist had pointed out that so far he hadn't touched on the plight of working-class women during the period in question. He'd said that this was history's omission, not his, but although this seemed to satisfy his questioner at the time, Lockhart now felt that he'd passed the buck. If he knew anything about history, he knew that people usually blamed it for their own failures.

So although it was a warm evening and he itched to be out, he rooted out a book with a token chapter on the plight of the wives and conscientiously slogged his way through it, taking notes. While he was doing so an image of his mother from an old black and white snapshot floated into his mind: wearing her nylon housecoat and with her hair tied up in a headscarf, she was leaning out of the window of their council house and wagging a warning finger at whoever was taking the picture.

Flicking through the book to look at some of the illustrations, Lockhart paused at one of a typical working-class interior, with the clothes-pulley above the range and the bed in the recess. Meant to illustrate privation, the solid and cosy look of the room made him think of his own modernized little flat with repugnance and long for the long-demolished home of his childhood. It was then that he'd looked up at the bare walls of his classroom and so he'd started – photographs, facsimiles, anything he could find to brighten the place up a bit. The simple pleasure of decoration had engrossed him and for the first time this term he'd been able to forget about time. He'd had to sprint for the train into town.

Emerging from the station in Edinburgh, he looked for a taxi but any he saw were taken. The streets were crowded because there had been a game on, and packs of drunken supporters roamed around chanting and singing. Most pubs were on the point of closing and people were spilling into the streets, less anxious to get home than usual because it was a warm night. Lockhart dodged between the revellers, wielding a weighty briefcase. He decided to take the long way home and stop in somewhere for a late pint, but the one or two pubs still serving were packed to the gills.

Almost home, he turned the corner into his street and barely avoided stepping on an enormously fat woman who lay on her back across the pavement, howling loudly. Her friend, a tight-lipped blonde with no-nonsense eyes, leaned over her and yanked at an arm.

'Ah'm warnin ye Margaret, get up!'

Margaret rolled around on the pavement, trapped in her outrageous distress, and howled some more. As Lockhart steered his way round her, the friend caught him by the arm. He jumped, as if electrocuted, and raised the briefcase as a barrier between them. She hung on tightly to his sleeve. His impulse was to shake himself free – he was on his way home and it had been a tiring day – but the earnestness in her eyes held him where he was.

'Ye've got to help me, gimme a hand to get *her* on her feet.'

She yanked her thumb at the fallen woman. Lockhart hummed and hawed, then reluctantly leaned his briefcase against the wall and said he'd try.

'Right then Margaret. This gentleman's gonnae help ye up – so *move* yersel, or else!'

Together they heaved in vain. Margaret went on rolling in her pain, heedless of anything else, howling inconsolably.

'What's the matter with her?'

'She's upset.'

As if that explained everything. Lockhart didn't pursue it. The main thing was to get her on her feet and get home, but as soon as they'd succeeded in raising her from the ground, she sagged and sat back down. Added to the weight of her weight, there was the ponderous burden of her reluctance. Abandoned to her howling, she had become oblivious to her surroundings and didn't notice a group of supporters on the other side of the street, jeering and catcalling. Her short black skirt had ridden up around her hips, exposing moons of white flesh between her stocking-tops and her knickers. The friend held a skinny finger out in front of Margaret's tear-stained and convulsing face, then yanked at her lank black hair.

'Margaret, Ah'm warnin you, if ye dinnae get a grip—'

'Come on, Margaret, time to go home!'

The fallen Margaret paused not to listen but to gasp for air and go on howling. The friend grabbed her face in one hand, pressing her fingers deeply into the loose flesh of the cheeks and shaking it violently. She slapped the howling woman hard and yelled:

'Move!'

'Don't hit her! Let me talk to her!'

'Ye're welcome! Go ahead and try!'

As he leaned over the howling woman to do so, a bead of

her bright blood dropped on to his shirt-cuff. Blood was trailing from her nose and running into her open mouth as she howled. The friend crouched beside him and dabbed at Margaret's face with a handkerchief.

'Look at what you've done!'

'She asked for it!'

Between her swollen eyelids, Margaret's brimming eyes seemed to gaze uncomprehendingly at Lockhart's face for a moment as she gasped for breath. She gazed at the blood-stained handkerchief, but if she saw it at all, it merely confirmed that she'd been deeply abused and so she howled all the more.

Lockhart squeezed her hot hand and tried to reason her out of her grief, every so often looking over his shoulder to see if anyone was looking.

'Listen to me, Margaret, I don't know what's wrong with you, I mean I don't know what's upset you so much, but whatever it was isn't worth it and you just can't lie here in the street like this. In the morning everything'll seem different, you'll see! So I think you should get up now and let your friend take you home! I'll help you!'

The friend yelled in Margaret's ear:

'Hear that, Margaret? This gentleman's gonnae help ye hame, so *move* or we're gonnae dump ye here!'

But Margaret had dumped herself here and had howled herself beyond the reach of reason or threat. Heaving her into a sitting position and propping her against the wall, Lockhart and the friend now hooked her under the armpits and wrenched her to her feet. Though the wall helped to support her, she lurched and wobbled unpredictably. Her feet flopped around like landed fish, then one of her shoes flipped off. Lockhart reached down to retrieve it – an absurdly dainty creation in red patent leather – then he felt Margaret come down on him.

Compressed against the wall, one hand holding aloft the shoe and the other hand trapped beneath a wide thigh, Lockhart let out a high, panicky laugh. The friend yanked, slapped, threatened and kicked. Margaret rolled over on her side and went on howling. Lockhart sprang to his feet and reached for his briefcase.

'Look, I'm sorry, but I have to get home.'

But the friend caught him by the lapel and pulled him face to face with her.

'Ye cannae leave me like this! Help me get her back to the flat! Help me an Ah'll gie ye what ye want!'

Lockhart wondered what she thought he wanted. He shook his head and picked up his briefcase.

'It's no far – please!'

'OK. One more try!'

Again they heaved. Suddenly, like Sisyphus on the crest of the hill, they were moving and gaining momentum. Their steps at first slow became comically rapid as they veered across the street.

Half-way across, Lockhart felt his legs give way under him and saw the ground rolling over his head. As they fell, the briefcase burst open and a pile of unmarked essays spilled out over the street. A taxi rounded the corner and screeched to a stop, blaring its horn at them. Seeing the 'FOR HIRE' sign, Lockhart jumped to his feet and waved his arms about. The driver looked him up and down and shook his head. Lockhart staggered to the driver's window and pleaded:

'Look, I don't know these people, but one of them's in a bad way and we've got to get her home.'

He pointed at Margaret, who was howling into his open briefcase, her bloodied cheek stuck to the first page of someone's essay, her hand flailing at a pile of the others.

'Her? No way.'

The friend stuck her head in the driver's window and swore at him. Lockhart pulled her away and stuck his own head in, tugging pound notes from his wallet.

'I'll make it worth your while.'

The driver eyed him with contempt and leaned on his horn. Margaret reared her head and responded with hers. The friend shouted abuse at her. Lockhart wrung his hands and begged.

'That's all very well, but what happens at the other end? Who gets her out the taxi and in her door?'

'I do,' said Lockhart. He felt the friend pressing against him and squeezing his arm. Finally the driver sighed with professional weariness and told them to make it snappy.

The décor made him think of a lounge bar, with its embossed maroon-and-gold wallpaper, the black leatherette sofa, the white wrought-iron coffee table with the glass top, the electric fire with the fibreglass coal and simulated flames and the artificial sheepskin rug. What had he expected – a clothes-pulley above the range? No, but maybe something more like his parents' living-room as he remembered it, with the solid wooden sideboard and the three-piece suite and the china cabinet in the corner. Looking round the room, he found the authentic detail he wanted: in an alcove to the side of the feature fireplace, three ducks were flying in a diagonal line.

Maureen – she'd told him her name in the taxi, leaning into him on a corner – was undressing Margaret and putting her to bed in a narrow box-room next door. It had taken half an hour to get here. Once inside the taxi, Margaret had stopped howling and fallen asleep, like an enormous baby lulled to sleep by the motion of the pram. It had taken ages to manoeuvre her out of the taxi and up the three flights of stairs to Maureen's flat. On the way up, she'd woken up and started howling again. A teenage girl who had been babysitting Maureen's son had opened the door to them. Now she seemed to have gone. Margaret was howling still and every so often he could hear Maureen cursing her as she struggled to put her to bed.

He spread out the soiled essays and notes over the coffee table to see which were salvageable. The door opened and a fair-haired boy of seven or eight stood there clutching a Hero Turtle.

'Hello there.'

The boy didn't answer, but stared at Lockhart with big, serious eyes – the likeness was clear. The boy eyed the briefcase and the papers spread out over the table.

'Are you C.I.D.?'

Lockhart laughed nervously.

'No, I'm a teacher.'

'A real yin?'

'I think so.'

'Ye are not.'

'I am so.'

'Prove it.'

Before Lockhart could try, the boy had gone, chopping him up with an imaginary sword as he went and shouting:

'I hate teachers!'

He heard Maureen yelling at the boy to tell him to get back to his bed, then some whispering – a deal of some kind was being made between mother and son in the hall – then she came into the room carrying a half-bottle of whisky and two empty glasses. She had taken her coat off and he saw that she was wearing a black dress gathered at one shoulder toga-style and held at the waist by an ornamental belt of silvery hoops.

'You're ma friend for life, George, honest.'

She sat down beside him and opened the whisky. She poured two huge measures and passed him one. They clinked glasses and drank.

'Let's have some music, eh?'

She half-walked, half-danced across the floor to the music centre. She ran her finger down a rack of cassettes and chose one. A slow, smoochy number oozed from the speakers. Maureen swayed to the rhythm of it as she walked towards him. She smoothed her skirt out at the back before she sat down.

'What's aw this then, yer homework or what?'

'Some essays I had to mark.'

'They're marked now, eh? You a teacher?'

'Your boy doesn't seem to think so. He wouldn't believe me.'

'Ye don't look the teacher type. He hates the school, hates the teachers.'

'I know, he told me.'

'He's a cheeky wee swine so he is, takes after his dad.'

Lockhart looked towards the door uneasily. Maureen laughed and nudged him.

'Dinnae worry aboot *him*, he left me six year ago.'

'I'm sorry.'

'Don't be. Better off withoot him.'

'I see.'

'I've worked for everythin Ah've got. Everythin ye see in this room. That carpet, that fireplace, this settee.'

She spread the fingers of one hand and patted the sofa, then she placed the hand on his shoulder, tilted her head, wagged her shoe and began to hum along to the music.

'Are ye gonnae put away yer homework, or what?'

As he did, a loose page fell from the pile of papers and Maureen bent down to pick it up. Her dress was short, and Lockhart glimpsed the long space between her thighs. She looked over her shoulder at him and smiled.

It was on, it was definitely on.

Maureen picked up the page, smoothed it out on the coffee table, frowned and read:

'The plight of working-class women. Margaret kens aboot that!'

'What's wrong with her?'

'What isnae?'

She rolled her eyes and handed him the piece of paper. He stuffed it into the briefcase with the others. He'd have to sort them out later, tell the class he'd been in an accident, these things happened.

'Yes, but what got her so upset?'

She groaned and refilled her glass, moving closer to him so that he could feel the pressure of her thigh against his. Lockhart squirmed a little to give his erection more room.

'Well, it's a long story but basically what happened is that Margaret got her books at the brewery, that's where she was workin, in the bottlin plant. Some job that – talk aboot soul-destroyin? Ah used tae work there masel, so Ah know what it's like, believe me. Now Ah'm in the office, Ah took a course on shorthand and typin, so it's no sae bad. Anyway, two days efter she gets her books, she gets a letter frae Northern Ireland an Dennis – that's her fiancé – says he's decided tae break it off wi her because o how he's no ready tae settle doon yet an aw that. He's in the army like. An the thing is tae, she thinks she might be pregnant, because he was back on leave a few weeks ago an she hasnae had a period yet. Then, tae put the tin lid on it, she gets tellt tae leave her digs for bein behind wi the rent, so Ah says tae her never mind, men are bad bastards the lottae them anyway, so Ah says she can kip in the box-room for a bit, till she gets hersel a new place an a job an that. So that's what's wrong wi her. She's depressed. She's been depressed since she moved in here. So the night Ah says tae her, come on Margaret, you'n me are gonnae go an have a night on the toon, but we didnae get as far as the disco. She wis knockin them back in the pub, drunk as a skunk, then some guys start tryin tae chat us up, complete arseholes, an yin asks her what circus she's in – the fat lady. That was enough for Margaret. She just started bubblin. Talk aboot a red face? Ah was mortified. Then in the street, she just couldnae stop howlin, Ah donno what Ah'd've done if you hadnae come along!'

As he leaned forward to put his glass down he felt her fingers stroke his neck loosely.

'What about you, eh? You married?'

'Divorced.'

'Kids?'

'One. A boy.'

'So we're in the same boat then, eh?'

Lockhart nodded. Maureen took his hand and stood up.

'Let's dance, eh?'

Lockhart took his jacket off and let it fall on the couch. Then they were holding each other close and moving very slowly round the dim room, her head resting on his shoulder, his hands moving down her back. When the number finished they were down on the sheepskin. It had been a long time for Lockhart, and an even longer time since he'd done it like this, on the rug in front of the fire. When he suggested that they go to bed, Maureen smiled at him with a kind of relieved resignation, then she took him through to her room.

The room was small and made to seem smaller by Maureen's gigantic bed – a relic of her marriage? – which had fitted bedside tables and a padded headboard. Lockhart undressed quickly and climbed in while she went to the toilet and switched things off next door.

When she came in she was wearing a black camisole, with suspenders and stockings – the works. She sat down on the bed, slid open a drawer and took out a contraceptive and a candle. She lit the candle, swearing as she spilled a spot of hot wax on her wrist, and stuck it in a candlestick. She turned in the bed to face him. She tore open the packet, took the condom out, then deftly unrolled it over his cock. He entered her slowly and soon they were moving in rhythm together. It quickly became an urgent, desperate fuck as their mutual hunger became clear, but something began to intrude. It was Margaret – she had started up again, sobbing and howling in the box-room. Maureen gripped his shoulders harder and told him to forget her, that she'd settle down soon, then they went on – all the more urgently, it seemed, because of the distraction in the background. It reminded him of the times with Elaine, when Ben had been a baby – chasing the orgasm had been like running for cover from the baby's cries. At her climax, Maureen cried out with what sounded like exasperation. He let himself come a moment later, surprised at the ease of it. He pulled out and lay on his back beside her. Maureen coughed harshly as she tried to catch her breath.

'I should cut down on the fags.'

'Me too.'

'Want one?'

'I'll share one.'

As they smoked, they listened to Margaret's grief, sometimes muffled by the pillow, sometimes spilling out of her freely in long, ululant howls.

'Ah wish she'd fucking shut up.'

'She can't help it.'

And obviously she couldn't help it. Long after Maureen had turned over on her side, pulled the covers up over her ears and fallen asleep, Lockhart went on listening to it, until it sounded the strangest thing on earth, this woman sobbing her heart out in the box-room next door, unsuppressible syllables of something which couldn't speak, had never found words for its condition. Even as he drifted into sleep he could still hear it, that something that couldn't speak, swelling and subsiding, voicing its elongated vowel of despair from century to century.

Where I'm From

'Where is this?'

Before answering his son, George Lockhart pulled up alongside a disused shop. Above its boarded-up window, painted letters spelled out 'NEWSAGE' – the remainder of the legend was hidden by an eczema of shredded posters and a rash of graffiti.

'This is where I'm from, Ben. That's called Arkin's Park.'

'Doesn't look like a park.'

Lockhart had to admit that his son had a point. The neglected space behind the solitary shop could hardly be called a park. The grassy expanse Lockhart remembered had shrunk to a mean corner of overgrown wasteground. Off in the distance, beyond the railway, there was nothing. There was just an emptiness where once the silhouette of the pit wheel had risen above a dark bing.

'I admit it's not how I remember it.'

Lockhart imagined himself as a boy: the unkempt, straw-coloured hair hanging over one eye. The skinny, suntanned arms and shoulders. The dirty, faded jeans and tee-shirt. In one hand, a grey tennis ball – every now and again he would bounce it on the ground, or throw it up in the air and catch it with ease. It had felt so right to throw that ball up in the air and catch it. He had refined it, so that he could catch the ball behind his back. In the other hand, a stick, both weapon and pencil. He could threaten people with it and draw things in the dirt.

In the middle of the wasteground stood a brick shed with a rusted corrugated iron roof and a padlocked door.

'What are we stopping here for?'

Lockhart pulled out his cigarette packet and held it up.

'You know you can't when I'm in the car, it's bad for my irritation.'

'I'm getting out. Coming?'

'I don't want to get out.'

Lockhart turned to look at his son. The boy was slumped in the seat, his heavy spectacles askew on his nose, a baseball cap drooping over one ear, the earphones of his personal stereo dangling around his neck. On the seat beside him there was a stack of sci-fi comics. Because of the skin problem his face looked permanently flushed, with an opaque quality that seemed to mask any expression. Overweight, strapped in the seat-belt, wired to his machine, with his stack of comics, he made Lockhart think of a sullen invalid wheeled out into the sun against his will.

He'd been looking after Ben for the past week. During the school holidays, he and Elaine, his ex-wife, looked after him week-about. He'd be taking Ben back to her place – it had once been his place too – in an hour or so. In a few days, Elaine was taking him on holiday with her to Greece, so this was Lockhart's last day with his son for a while.

He'd taken him lots of places, maybe too many, over the past week. He regretted bringing him here, especially on their last afternoon. His idea had been to show him something – where his father came from, where his grandparents had lived – in the hope that this would give him a stronger sense of something: his background, himself.

They had stopped first at the primary school, but it had been long since closed and converted into a block of flats. He had taken Ben around the playground – now a car park –

pointing out what he could, remembering small events of his own childhood, and had been dismayed by his son's patent indifference. Then he'd driven to a new housing estate which had been a cornfield when he was a boy. He turned the car around and drove away, telling him about how they had hidden themselves in the corn to share their plunder of stolen apples, how they'd used a corner of the field as a racetrack for their bikes and as a football ground. He'd even remembered how sometimes, as it was getting dark, an older boy – dressed for the dancing in suit, shirt and tie – would join in the game for a few minutes before strutting off into the night. He'd tried to explain to him that this was a kind of ritual, that the boy wasn't just showing off his new suit, but was having a last kick of the ball, a last shot at childhood before meeting the new, more threatening game of the dance hall. Ben had listened dutifully but none of it had prompted his curiosity. By the time he had found the house where he'd been born, Ben had started whining to go home.

'Tell you what. I'll get out, go for a walk, have a smoke. You can stay here, OK?'

'Not on my own.'

Lockhart smacked the back of the passenger seat with the palm of his hand and cursed.

'So what do you suggest?'

'Open a window.'

Lockhart shook his head in exasperation, shrugged and cranked the window down. When he lit the cigarette, Ben coughed sarcastically and scratched at his peeling skin.

'What did we come here for? You said we were going for a drive.'

'We've been for a drive.'

'You didn't say we were coming here.'

'I thought you might be interested to see where I grew up, where your grandparents lived, but obviously I was wrong.'

If Ben felt any interest his eyes betrayed no flicker of it. He fiddled with his digital watch, making it emit a tiny repertoire of buzzes and bleeps.

'Did you hear me? This is where I grew up.'

'I heard.'

Ben ejected his cassette, turned it over, pressed the 'play' button and manoeuvred the earphones on to his head. Lockhart found himself shouting:

'Switch that damn thing off!'

He yanked the earphones from the boy's head. Ben let out a high whine of outrage, then his face buckled into an ugly caricature of anguish as he cried loudly and deliberately, his pale eyes overflowing.

'Shut up!'

But Ben went on howling with abandon.

'You're not a baby, for christsake! Switch that damn thing off!'

Ben stopped crying as suddenly as he had started, rubbed his eyes with the sleeve of his shirt, then stabbed at the 'stop' button with his thumb.

'Don't you think at your age, you should stop having tantrums? Don't you think it's time you grew up?'

'Time you grew up yourself!'

Lockhart threw his head back to declare a scathing laugh.

'See that shop there?'

Ben glanced at it briefly, then looked glumly at his father. His watery blue eyes, made unnaturally large by the thick lenses of his spectacles, looked vaguely affronted.

'Every morning before school and every afternoon after school, on my bike, I delivered the newspapers for that shop. On Saturday I delivered the late pink final and on Sunday the Sunday papers. It was a seven-day week, Ben, and I handed over that money to my mother—'

'Late pink what?'

'Final. The late edition of the paper was printed on pink paper.'

'Why pink?'

Sometimes his son's curiosity irritated him as much as his indifference.

'I don't know, it just was.'

'Can we go now?'

'See that building there? Guess what that was used for when I was a boy, Ben.'

Ben barely glanced at the grim brick shed with the rusty roof before sighing emphatically and answering:

'Search me.'

'Scout hut.'

He had thought this might interest him, since Ben was keen on the Scouts.

'What a dump.'

Lockhart stubbed out his cigarette and cranked up the window.

'Are we going now?'

'I want to show you one more thing.'

'What?'

'The pit where my dad – your grandad – worked.'

'I don't want to see it.'

Lockhart gripped the steering wheel tightly.

'OK. Get out.'

Though he didn't look round he could sense his son looking up at him with alarm.

'Go on, get out. Some fresh air'll do you good. I'll be half an hour at most. You can wait for me.'

'*Here?*'

'If you go past that hut and over the other side, there's a path that runs alongside the railway. Go along it till you reach

a bridge. Over the bridge, there's a swingpark. I'll meet you
back here in half an hour.'

'I'm too old for swingparks.'

'Since when?'

'Since last year.'

'Because you started at high school, is that it? Just because
you're a whizz at computer games, you think you're too smart
to enjoy a swing?'

'The sun's bad for my skin.'

'So don't take off your shirt, turn your cap round the right
way so the peak keeps your face in shade. You can't let a bit
of sun defeat you.'

He had given this or similar advice on countless occasions.
He no longer had to think about the words, and he was sure
Ben no longer listened. It had become a kind of routine
between them.

'I'm not getting out. I'll come to the pit with you.'

'No you won't. You're not interested, so what's the point?'

Lockhart leaned over and unfastened his son's safety-belt.
The boy glared at him.

'You heard me, Ben. Out.'

'But Dad—'

'No buts. Out you get.'

Ben looked at him in disbelief, the wide, shallow pools of
his eyes threatening to spill their tears again. Even as he
lumbered out of the car he kept his eyes on his father, as if
expecting him to smile, tell him he was joking and that he
should get back in.

Lockhart pulled the door shut and waved Ben away with a
hand. As he watched his son step awkwardly into the area of
wasteground behind the shop he felt an acute and useless pity
for him.

He started up the engine, giving it too much gas, and drove

away. As soon as he'd turned the corner he began to feel bad. He'd caused the argument, by expecting his son to be interested in something which was too abstract and remote for him to imagine – his father's background.

He had lost the will to go and look at the pit himself. Anyway, he knew it would be a flattened site. He would drive around for five minutes, then go back for Ben.

On the way to Elaine's, Lockhart tried to make amends. He asked about the planned holiday to Greece, the Scouts, his fossil collection, his friends at school, the music he liked listening to, the sci-fi comics he was so keen on. Ben answered the questions reluctantly. Only when the sci-fi comics were mentioned did he seem to betray any real interest. Lockhart listened to the names of the comics he liked best, and was treated to a summary of some of the stories – more intricate than he'd have suspected – and one story in particular:

'It's about this alien race called the Numen who have to leave their planet because it's invaded by the triludans . . .'

He was relieved to draw up outside Elaine's ground-floor flat in Edinburgh. He got Ben's bag out of the car and carried it up the path to the door. Ben followed him. He rang the bell, but there was no answer.

'I'll get it.'

Lockhart was surprised that his son had his own key to the door. He watched him open the door and hold it open for him before stepping inside.

It was the first time he'd stepped inside for a while. More often than not, he dropped Ben at Elaine's door and she at his. The hall had been redecorated and he stood in the middle of it uneasily, reluctant to go any further.

'Are you coming through, or what?'

Ben opened the kitchen door and waited for him.

'I'll stay till Elaine gets back.'

In the kitchen, Ben switched on the kettle and asked him if he wanted coffee. Lockhart nodded, sat down and watched him. His son had suddenly become animated. Maybe he was just pleased to be home. This was his home, no matter how often he came to stay at his place.

'So where is she? She was supposed to be here by now.'

Ben shrugged.

'She'll be back. You can go if you want. I'll be OK.'

'I'm not in any hurry, I'll wait.'

Ben made him coffee, then busied himself around the kitchen – opening the fridge, pouring himself a glass of juice, making a peanut-butter sandwich. He seemed eager to talk.

'Dad? You know that place we went today?'

'Uh huh.'

'Is that really where you grew up?'

'Yes. What about it?'

Ben was tilting his head and looking at him strangely.

'You don't go there any more though, do you?'

'Well, no. Today was the first time for years.'

'Why not?'

'Hmm?'

'If you like it so much, why don't you go there more?'

'I never said I liked it. I just said it was where I grew up.'

Ben sat down at the kitchen table opposite him and appeared to consider this seriously while he chewed his sandwich. He stopped chewing to ask:

'What did you leave it for?'

'I left when I went to college.'

Ben nodded slightly, as if this made sense, and said:

'That was what Mum said.'

'What?'

'That's why she left the place where she grew up. She took me there the weekend before last.'

Lockhart spluttered on his coffee, then laughed.

'She took you to Fort William? You're kidding!'

Ben nodded once and took another bite.

'That must've been great for you. Fort William! The centre of the Universe!'

Ben stopped chewing, held his glass of juice half-way to his mouth and looked at Lockhart steadily.

Lockhart started back-pedalling:

'I don't really mean that, I know it's where Mum's from—'

Ben interrupted him quickly, wagging the crust of his sandwich in the air:

'It's a dump.'

'Maybe it doesn't seem that way to her. Anyway, why did she take you there? It's not as if she has relatives or friends there now—'

'Neither do you.'

'What?'

'You don't know anybody in the place you grew up either, do you?'

'Well, no, I suppose you're right, but Fort William's a lot further away.'

'Only in miles.'

Lockhart, taken aback by the perspicacity of this, could only mutter his agreement.

'Anyway Dad, I thought where you grew up was a worse dump than Fort William.'

'You're right.'

They heard the key in the front door and Ben jumped off his chair and ran to meet his mother. Lockhart stood up, stepped into the hall and stopped there when he saw Elaine. She was bending down to hug Ben and she had a parcel under one arm. She looked at him and said breathlessly:

'Sorry I'm late. There was a traffic jam—'

He shrugged and waved a hand loosely to say it didn't matter. He moved from foot to foot as she turned back to Ben, who was pawing at the parcel. When she laughed, Lockhart felt the slight queasiness of remembered happiness, remembered desire.

'I think it's what you wanted. Here.'

Ben took the parcel and ran with it into his room. Elaine straightened up and looked directly at him.

'So. How has it been?'

'OK, I think. I think he's glad to be home.'

'For a day or two, then it'll be: "When's Dad coming to take me?"'

Lockhart shook his head and smiled at the suggested compliment. He looked at his ex-wife. She brushed a loose strand of hair away from her eyes and smiled at him. She looked attractive to him, but tense. She had always been tense.

'How are you, Elaine?'

'All right. Busy. You know what it's like.'

He nodded.

'I suppose I'd better go. I hope the holiday goes well.'

'We'll send you a postcard.'

Something made him pull her to him and embrace her. She was slightly surprised, but only slightly. He had done it often enough since their separation. He held her tightly, too tightly for the occasion. He wanted to tell her how hard he had been finding it without her, but as he raised his eyes he saw Ben framed in the bedroom doorway, brandishing his present. It was some kind of laser gun. He had forgotten about it as he looked at them embracing. They broke apart, but didn't let go of each other completely, to face him. Lockhart saw the look of mingled hope and hurt in his son's eyes. It was the boy who spoke:

'This planet is where I'm from. What a dump!'

He exterminated them in a cacophony of zooms and zaps, in a blaze of fluorescent, strobic light.

Not about the Kids

He could just remember the apples and oranges careering around the kitchen. And the grapes – that's right, he'd just bought those grapes in the afternoon. He'd picked up a bunch of them in the fruit shop and felt their luxurious weight in his hand, half wondering if he could really afford them, what with being unemployed, and half thinking that the kids hardly ever got grapes. The way they'd scattered all over the floor, ricocheting around the kitchen like the beads of a broken necklace! In his anger he'd scooped the fruitbowl off the table and, in one sweeping movement, flung it at the wall. It had exploded into a fountain of blue glass and a wild eruption of fruit. Thank Christ the kids had been in the bath. He had to make sense of what had happened, or else here he was, driving through the night with no real clue about why he was here, in the middle of nowhere in Fife.

A light rain was beginning to fall and he switched on the wipers. He stared at the road in front of him. He was driving. He had to keep his mind on the road. It felt like he'd been driving for a long time, for years and years of his life. Now the road seemed to come at him out of the night, negotiating him rather than the other way round. If he could just concentrate on driving this car along this road, maybe all the other stuff would sort itself out. He'd had a row with his wife and now he was driving. That was all there was to it. But what was it about?

He braked to take a corner and heard the grinding screech of metal on metal. The brake-pads needed to be changed months ago. Now the discs would be scuppered. The shocks needed to be replaced as well, and one of the rear coil-springs was broken. Age, the guy at the garage had told him, looking at him rather than the car. But he hadn't had the money to go and get the work done there and then. At any moment the broken spring could leap out, and the car collapse on to the rear axle.

It had been something so trivial, of course, not about the kids but about the housework – the household chores! Ruth had made a comment about putting the rubbish out – was that how it had started? He'd been sitting there at the table, after the communal family meal. Bobby had been obstreperous as usual, throwing his food on the floor, insisting on drinking out of a glass like everyone else, then spilling his juice all over the table. Emma had been finicky and difficult and the food – an experimental fish curry – hadn't gone down well. There had been a bottle of wine – his idea, along with the grapes. Ruth had declined the wine wearily, saying it was a waste of money. Maybe it had started with the wine, with the waste of money.

When the table had been cleared, with Bobby on his knee, popping a grape or two into the boy's mouth, he'd been aware of Ruth making more of a thing of doing the dishes than usual. The plates were crashing and colliding in the sink and she was smashing handfuls of cutlery down on the metal draining board. He'd asked her what was wrong with her. Nothing, she'd said, but in a tone of voice that seethed with resentment. Then she'd started sweeping the kitchen floor and shouting at Emma to get out from under her feet.

When he thought about it now, it came clearer that what he'd been trying to do was to woo her, but he'd tried to include the kids. What was needed was not about the kids.

What was needed was something else. It was as if she held him responsible for trying but failing, as if the attempt had reminded her of how things should be but were not. The way she'd swept that floor, like some vengeful Cinderella.

Leave it, he'd said, just leave it and I'll do it later on. Then she'd started dealing with the rubbish, tugging that black bag out of the bucket, tying it up so tightly ... What was she trying to tell him? Had he been neglecting this twice-weekly household ritual, normally earmarked as a chore of his in the demarcation of labour between them? She'd deliberately done one of his chores, encroached on his territory, so that she could get at him about it – could this be true?

He'd picked up Bobby and grabbed Emma by the arm and made for the door. Ruth had shouted something at him about the way he was handling the kids. He'd shouted back: No, this has nothing to do with the kids! So he'd removed them from the battlefield, running their bath and putting them in it before returning to wage war with Ruth about the rubbish. He'd tried to take over but she'd resisted and they'd ended up having a tug-of-war with the rubbish bag. It had split and all the food scraps and nappies and tin cans and eggshells had spilled over the floor, the floor she'd just swept. They'd stopped everything then to argue savagely. He'd smashed the fruitbowl and stamped out of the house, slamming the door. It was awful, it was desperate ... But what was it all about?

He was finding it hard to concentrate on driving. He didn't know this road and it kept surprising him, dipping and rising and twisting into the night unpredictably. He couldn't go back tonight, that was for certain. Maybe this time he wouldn't go back at all. Maybe this was it. Maybe they'd both remember this night like no other night in their lives.

Up ahead, just beyond the range of his dipped headlights, there was some kind of truck. One of its brake-lights wasn't working. A truck or a lorry? It was hard to make out in the dark. The way it seemed to veer from side to side unpredictably at every bend bothered him. He put his foot on the accelerator. He felt his heartbeat speeding up. If Ruth had been with him he wouldn't take the risk – but she wasn't.

Before he could get level he saw, above the dark embankment, the light from an approaching car's headlights. He braked and pulled back in. The bastard hadn't slowed down to let him pass – hadn't he stepped on it to make sure he couldn't? The approaching car dipped its headlights as it came round the corner. Even so, it dazzled him and he slowed down till it had passed. There was a moment when he could make out nothing but the brake-light of the truck, dancing around in the night ahead, a taunting spark. This road was wild. It wasn't so much the blind summits or the hairpin bends, but the stretches in between, where the road wavered and couldn't make up its mind which way to go. It was a dangerous road. Maybe it didn't go anywhere.

He came over a rise and saw the truck there ahead, its one brake-light jiggling up and down, its back-plate rattling. It had slowed down. He accelerated and signalled to overtake, but it was taking longer than it should. The truck threw a spray of dirty rainwater over his windscreen and snarled at him as he drew level with it. He could feel the car jogging around on the uneven road. It was a relief to get in front. He put his foot down and tried to leave it behind.

A sharp bend in the road came at him and he had to brake hard to get round it. The brakes screeched. The car skidded and swung too far into the side of the road and scraped noisily against the barrier beneath the sign with the chevrons. At the same moment he was dazzled by the headlights of an oncoming car and he raised his right hand to shield his eyes, trying to right the wheel with his left hand. The other car roared past blaring its horn. His heart was hammering and he could feel his hands and his arms shaking. He had to stop somewhere as soon as possible.

As if the road had taken this decision, it wound downwards and showed him a speed-limit sign and the nameplate of a village he'd never heard of. He saw a pub just off the main street, then pulled over and waited till the truck roared past. It was just a truck, moving something from somewhere to somewhere else in the night, but it had seemed to him an enemy. He put his hand to his head, pressing his thumb and his forefinger into his eyelids, and he sat like this for a moment before switching off the engine and the lights.

There were only a few people in the pub and he was conspicuous as he walked to the bar. He was a stranger, and they didn't often get strangers here. They stared at him with hostile curiosity. Some of them seemed to dismiss him quickly, as if they knew he'd just had a row with his wife.

The barman took too long to serve him. He was having a conversation with some of the men sitting round the bar. Apparently they were talking about birds, birds they found living in the eaves of their houses. One man was maintaining that when swifts made their nests they used their spit to hold them together, and that swift's spit was the main ingredient in bird's-nest soup.

He ordered a double and asked if there was a phone. The barman pointed to the door that led to the toilets. He took his drink to a table by the window, drank half of it and smoked a cigarette. He thought about what he should say to her.

Ruth, it was the way you swept the floor.

Ruth, I demand custody of the kids.

Ruth, I think you should have custody of the kids. They can come to me half the week and stay with you the other half.

Ruth, we need to talk. Not about the kids. About us. What's happening to *us*, Ruth?

He looked at the only woman in the bar, as if this might help him to think of what he should say to his wife. She was sitting on a high stool up at the bar, next to a man – her husband? She wore a tailored leather jacket, the collar of which she held between her finger and thumb to illustrate her point. The man shook his head, raised his eyebrows wearily and slouched on his stool, over which he'd slung his nylon jerkin. They seemed a sad couple, trapped in their coupledom. But maybe they weren't a couple at all. And if they were a couple – what did that mean, exactly, when you got down to it?

The others sitting at the bar all seemed to know each other, though some wore muddied work boots and dungarees, others sports jackets or suits. Over in the far corner, two younger men in jeans and tee-shirts were playing pool and listening to the juke-box.

He took his drink and his cigarettes out to the telephone with him. It was an old-fashioned phone. It felt unusual to dial his own number.

'It's me. Sorry about the fruitbowl.'

'So am I – not just about the fruitbowl.'

'I know it isn't just about that. I'll get another one exactly the same.'

'Like hell. It was antique.'

'I know, I know, it's irreplaceable. I was angry.'

'You were angry. Right. That explains everything. You were angry so you threw the fruitbowl at the wall.'

He apologized again then waited until she spoke.

'Where are you?'

'Fife.'

'What the hell are you doing there?'

'I don't know, I drove here.'

'You must be out of your mind.'

'I am. I am totally out of my mind.'

'You're drunk.'

'No, not yet.'

'You're driving.'

'That's right. I'm driving.'

'You must be crazy.'

'You're right. I must be.'

She didn't reply to that. He waited a minute, then he said:

'What's it all about?'

'What?'

'This. What's it all about?'

'What do you think it's all about?'

'That's what I'm asking you.'

She sighed with fatigue and said wearily that she didn't know. He was glad she didn't.

'It's something to do with me losing my job isn't it? Something else will turn up. It's got to.'

'It's not just that. What makes you think it's that?'

'I'm around the house too much. We're with each other all the time. I mean, sometimes a person has to go away just so that they can come back.'

'Don't come back. Not tonight.'

'Don't worry, I won't.'

'I don't want to talk. I'm tired, I want to go to bed.'

'I'll tell you a bedtime story, then. Once upon a time, there was a boy and a girl, and they fell madly in love with each other. But they were young, just kids—'

'I've heard it before.'

'Not this one, Ruth, this one is not about us, this one is about these kids, these kids who fell madly in love. We're talking about a time when people went out with each other for a fortnight, if it was serious. But these kids are so in love they manage to go on for a year, more than a year ... That gives you some idea how serious about each other they are. But, as I was saying, they're young, too young really to know how to *go on* being in love, if you know what I mean, and after a while something has to happen.'

The pips sounded, and he hurriedly pulled a handful of coins from his pocket, dumped them on the shelf and searched among them for a ten pence. He found one and put it in just as they were about to be cut off.

'So, and this is the sad bit of the story, there comes a point when the boy begins to feel restless, he feels the need for change ... He's changing anyway, he's growing up, and the whole world is changing round about him. And so one night, out of the blue, the boy tells the girl he wants to finish with her. So they split up. Some time passes. The boy is totally miserable without the girl. Then he goes back to her, and she takes him back with open arms. And they go on together again, pretty much as before except that everything has changed. In fact, nothing is ever quite the same after that brief separation. And soon the girl begins to feel restless, she feels the need for change ...'

'You got what you deserved. What d'you want, sympathy?'

'All I'm saying is sometimes people need the threat of separation, I mean so that they can go on. The threat has to be real. But as soon as it is real it will never go away, it will always be there. D'you know what I'm saying, Ruth?'

'You're saying it's time to split up.'

'I never said that.'

'Maybe we should.'

'Just remember it was you who suggested it first.'

'What does it matter who suggests it first?'

'It matters. Everything matters.'

'Don't sound so gloomy about it.'

'How should I sound – cheerful?'

'I'm not saying that.'

'What are you saying?'

'I'm not saying anything.'

'Well, why not? Are we communicating with each other here or what?'

'I don't want to communicate. I'm sick of communicating. We can communicate tomorrow.'

'What about tomorrow?'

But he could feel her attention slipping away from him. He tried to hold it:

'Are the kids OK?'

'They're asleep, if that's what you mean.'

'That isn't what I mean.'

'What do you mean then?'

'I mean are they OK? Come on, you know what I mean.'

'They're OK, yes.'

'Christ Ruth, I was trying tonight. I tried with the meal, I tried with the kids, I tried with us . . .'

'I know you tried. D'you think I haven't been trying? I'm always trying. Maybe that's the problem. Maybe it's just too much effort.'

'You sound exhausted, Ruth.'

'I am. My period's come.'

'D'you think that had something to do with it?'

'How do I know? Maybe, maybe not.'

The pips went. He tried to tell her that he'd call her again in the morning, but he was cut off.

He took his drink back to the bar, finished it and ordered another. No one seemed to pay him any attention now, and they had become a meaningless blur for him. He didn't want to look at them, so he sat down in a chair that faced the window. He stared at his distorted image reflected in the marbled glass, and when he moved his head a little, his features contorted horribly.

Her period? Maybe, maybe not. But what, really, had happened? Maybe nothing had really happened. Maybe the threat was all that was needed. But then, maybe what he'd said to her was true: once the threat was there, it would never really go away.

If she could be here with him now ... But all that lay ahead was the night, a night spent alone, in a bed-and-breakfast in Fife. The utter pointlessness of it made him bang his glass down on the table as he finished his drink. Someone laughed at the bar and he thought he heard a low-toned comment from one of the tables. He closed his eyes and listened. The clack of the pool balls, the music from the juke-box, the voices – all the noises in the bar seemed to swell inside him and engulf him, until he felt adrift in the world. He had to get out.

It had stopped raining, and the night was cool and clear. He walked to the car but didn't get in. He leaned against it and looked along the dark street of the village, at the haphazard silhouette of the rooftops. He imagined the swifts in the eaves, their nests held together with spit, their eggs ... It reminded him vaguely of his childhood, although he had never lived in such a place.

In a Dark Room with a Stranger

Although she had her back turned and he couldn't see her expression, he knew she was angry by the way she was frying the liver. He tried to sound casual:

'Where are you meeting Jane?'

'Wine bar.'

He pretended to yawn, stretching out his arms. He wanted her to look at him.

'I'm looking forward to a night in.'

She tossed her head briefly and made a dismissive noise as she breathed out. He knew he should let it pass, but her reaction angered him – wasn't it the latest in a long line of dismissals? – and he couldn't stop himself demanding:

'What's that supposed to mean?'

'What's what supposed to mean?'

'All I said was I was looking forward to a night in.'

'You've been out every night this week, that's all.'

'I have not.'

'Nearly every night. You were out drinking with Mike last night. You were out the night before and on Monday – you saw Mike on Monday as well.'

'That's three nights out of seven.'

'So far.'

'I'm staying in tonight. And tomorrow night. That makes three nights out of seven, Madeleine.'

Though what he was saying was reasonable, it was said

with a savage defiance.

'So?'

'That isn't every night.'

'It's two more than I'm having.'

'Where would we be without arithmetic? I'm not stopping you.'

'I don't want to go out three nights a week. We can't afford it.'

'Here we go. Money.'

'No wonder. You don't think about what you spend when you go out. Jenny needs a new coat for the winter. So does Lucy. And you said you'd decorate their room weeks ago.'

'What's that got to do with it?'

'You haven't even bought the wallpaper. These things cost money we haven't got. I mean, have you any idea what our balance is?'

'This service is unavailable. Please refer to your bank. All I say is I'm looking forward to a night in and I get a bank statement shoved down my throat.'

'Anyway, a night in will do your liver good.'

She stabbed at a wedge of the sizzling meat with a fork and cursed.

'Never mind my liver, that stuff's going to burn to a cinder if you're not careful.'

'I don't have time to be careful.'

'So we're having burnt liver for dinner. Great.'

'I bought liver to try and economize.'

This was said with open hostility and, for the first time during their conversation, she turned to face him. He stepped towards her and reached out to her but she pushed his hand away and turned back to the cooker.

'Madeleine, what's happening? We're like strangers.'

'No. Strangers would give each other more.'

'You're right.'

But the fact that she was right didn't help. Neither did this:

'No wonder I go out – what is there for me here?'

She glanced over her shoulder and looked hurt about that, then put the ball back in his court, telling him he'd made no effort whatsoever to communicate with her, to find out how she was feeling.

'The way you've been makes me feel you don't want me to.'

'The way I've been! What about the way you've been?'

That's how it had gone, on and on like that, with both arguing that it was the way the other had been. Then she'd turned a piece of the liver over too violently, so that the hot oil in the frying pan spattered her hand. Then she'd slammed the frying pan on the cooker, thrown the fork on the floor and rushed out of the room.

Lucy had started wailing in the other room and he'd had to go to her after switching off the gas under the burnt liver. She'd fallen and hit her head on the edge of the coffee table. Then Madeleine had come through, eyes wild with tears and mascara, and she'd told him he was useless with the kids. The argument had stopped there – Jenny had looked up from her drawing and told them to stop it – but the silence between them had grown through bathtime, storytime and bedtime.

The kids had picked up on it. Lucy had taken longer than usual to settle and her cries had been more urgent than the usual bedtime whimpers of reluctance. Then Jenny, during the bedtime story, had started asking him again about the business of not talking to strangers. She'd wanted to know if it was OK to talk to Mike when he came round to the house. He'd tried to explain to her that Mike wasn't a stranger, that he was a friend and that it was OK to talk to strangers when she was with somebody she knew, and so on ... But the whole business seemed to be bothering her and when reassurance failed he'd had to distract her with another bedtime story, so that by the time he'd got her to bed, Madeleine was walking out the door.

He pulled the newspaper over the kitchen table towards him and unfolded it. He'd bought it in the morning, on the way to the swingpark with Lucy. Sometimes it was possible to read a bit of the paper while he pushed her on the swing, but this morning she'd wanted out of the swing after a couple of minutes. He'd tried to read it again at lunchtime but that hadn't worked out either, because Jenny, back from her dance class, had wanted to talk: wasn't Miss Horner, the dance teacher, a stranger? He'd found it more difficult than it should have been to make out a case for Miss Horner not being a stranger, since he'd never met the woman and knew nothing about her, and his explanations only seemed to add to the confusion.

He filled the kettle and switched it on. Then, thinking he heard Jenny crying out – sometimes she woke up when he was thinking about her, as if the thought had activated some telepathic alarm button in her – he went to the room and looked in.

She was lying with her arms thrown above her head and her hair across her face. He pulled the cover up around her and moved the hair off her face as gently as he could. Before leaving the room he looked at the baby. She was sleeping soundly, but had moved around in the cot in such a way that one of her feet was sticking out between the bars. He re-arranged her position slowly, trying not to wake her. Before leaving her he looked at the faint, reddish swelling on her forehead where she'd bumped her head. It wasn't so bad, but it was going to be visible for at least a day. He closed the door quietly as he left the room.

Useless with the kids.

The insult of it made him pace up and down in the kitchen as he waited for the kettle to boil. Maybe she was right. He'd found the whole business about talking to strangers hard to handle. Maybe without the hangover, he now reflected, it would have been easier.

He shouldn't have met Mike again last night, having had a night with him already on the Monday. Even Mike hadn't particularly wanted to go out drinking. He'd more or less made Mike feel obliged to meet him. It was meant to be a quick drink, nothing more, but he'd insisted on buying another before Mike had had the chance to suggest leaving. After the first two drinks, the evening had run its course between them in the usual way. Mike was the same age, but single. He had a girlfriend, but she was Italian and at present in Italy. The meetings at airports, the travelling, the long periods of separation and the long-distance phone calls – though it all sounded glamorous to him, Mike was clearly sick of it. Mike wanted a nourishing family life. He thought he wanted kids.

In the end, it had been a good enough night, though they'd talked about Mike's problems with his relationship but not his problem with Madeleine. It was kind of assumed that because they lived together and had kids, everything was basically OK. Maybe everything basically was, but getting through the day with a hangover and having to deal with the kids and then the argument with Madeleine ... The day's little events crowded in on him and repeated themselves over and over in his mind – the way Lucy had squealed to get out of that swing; what Jenny had said about Miss Horner; that Peruvian woman he'd met on the bus, who'd told him she'd come to Scotland, fallen madly in love, the way she'd smiled at him, as if everything in life was as it should be! – until his life seemed worthless, seemed meaningless.

He made himself a mug of tea, sat down and stared at the newspaper. His hand shook a little when he went to lift the mug to his mouth, but the tea tasted reviving. He scanned the headlines and dipped into one of the front-page stories. It was about a child who'd been abducted, raped and murdered. He didn't like the way it was reported. There was a certain relish of the horror of what had happened. His own reaction bothered him. On the one hand, he felt that he would enjoy inflicting pain on such a man. His guts cried out for revenge. On the other hand, he thought that these people were the inevitable products of a screwed-up society and that they should be rehabilitated. The division between his heart and his head was disturbing.

The case had been in the news for the last few days. That was partly why the thing about strangers had come up with Jenny – they had both been warning her about strangers. It was important. But now that he had started reading the newspaper it felt like the wrong thing to be doing. He wasn't really reading it. There was something else he had to deal with that was more important.

He was still not really reading it when the phone rang. He'd moved it into the bedroom earlier, when he'd put the kids down, because when it rang in the hall it sometimes woke up the baby. He hurried through and answered it.

'Hello? Hello?'

Nobody answered, but he felt sure there was somebody there. It wasn't that he could hear someone's breathing; more that the silence felt like someone holding their breath.

'Hello.'

He was about to hang up when the person on the other end cleared his or her throat. The sound brought gooseflesh to the back of his neck. He couldn't tell if it was a man or a woman, but it sounded very near, almost as if he'd heard himself clearing his own throat.

'*Hello.*'

No answer. He wondered if he had maybe just imagined the throat-clearing, or that what he had thought was somebody clearing their throat had been some kind of interference on the line, but no – there was definitely someone there. He felt as if he was in a dark room with somebody, in a dark room with a stranger who had just come in, who was standing near him in the darkness, just standing a few feet away from him in the darkness, waiting.

'Who is it?'

It annoyed him that his own voice sounded falsely casual.

'It's me.'

He sighed with exasperation.

'Madeleine. What d'you want?'

'I want to talk to you.'

'Go ahead.'

'If you're going to be like that, I'll hang up.'

'Like what?'

'You know.'

'Well, what d'you want to say exactly?'

'Nothing *exactly*.'

That 'exactly' was a mistake. It had just slipped out. He tried to counteract it:

'Are you at the wine bar?'

'Yes. Jane isn't here yet.'

'Oh.'

There was a pause. He heard her lighting a cigarette and exhaling with fatigue.

'We really have to talk.'

'I was trying to talk to you earlier.'

'I mean, here I am, trying to have a night out for the first time for ages. And I can't enjoy it.'

'Why not?'

'You know why not.'

'Listen, I don't want it to be the way it is, believe me.'

'D'you think I do? I mean, d'you think I enjoy this?'

'All I know is this whole thing is wearing me out. I've had enough.'

'You've had enough! Don't you think I've had enough?'

Although there was agreement of a kind, both were still intent on stating their own case. He tried to come at it from another angle:

'We need to spend more time together.'

'If you didn't go out so much—'

'You've said that already.'

'Anyway, we're with each other too much – you said that the other day.'

'But not together. All I'm saying is maybe we need a night out together.'

'Or a night in.'

'A night in then, what difference does it make? You know what I'm talking about. I'm talking about us. I hate it when it's like this. The kids feel it too.'

'I know that. You don't have to tell me that.'

'Jenny keeps making me promise never to leave you and her and Lucy.'

'She said that to me when you went out last night.'

'She knows it can happen.'

'So do I.'

'She doesn't want it to happen.'

There was a pause, then she said softly:

'How about you?'

'Of course I don't. It's just that I get to the point where I don't know who I am. I'm just a parent. I feel like a stranger to myself.'

'Tell me about it. It's called baby-stress.'

'I know it is, but it's you and me too, Madeleine. If we don't fit together, everything else falls out of place.'

'This pattern keeps repeating itself.'

'That's because it's a repeating pattern, like on wallpaper.'

The wallpaper was a mistake. It had been niggling at him since she'd mentioned it earlier, but now he cursed himself inwardly for coming out with it.

'What?'

'Wallpaper.'

'What about wallpaper?'

'You know. A repeating pattern. I've been thinking. About the kids' room.'

'You've been thinking about it for three months.'

'I think I'll paint it.'

'For christsake, I didn't phone up to talk about decorating the kids' room.'

'I'm going to do it, Madeleine, it's just that I can't bring myself to buy the wallpaper. It's all so hideous.'

'They make some nice wallpaper for kids nowadays, you're looking in the wrong shops.'

'Why don't you buy it? Why do I always have to do these things?'

'All right, I'll buy the bloody wallpaper. I'll even put it up.'

'I'll put it up. If you get it.'

'Fine.'

'But I'd rather paint the room. It would be a damn sight quicker.'

'You'll still have to get the paint, choose the colours, borrow the ladders . . . It'll take you just as long.'

'Why can't Jenny choose the colours?'

'She'll want a completely pink room.'

'It's her room, not ours.'

'Anyway, we can talk about this another time. My money's running out.'

'Put some more money in then.'

'I haven't got any more change. Wait a minute. I've got one more ten pence—'

The line was interrupted briefly as she put the money in. He noticed that he was gripping the phone tightly and holding it so hard against his ear that it hurt. So this was it. If peace was to be restored, it had to be done now.

'Look. I'm sorry about earlier. Madeleine, I really want you to enjoy your night out.'

He heard her taking a drink and wished he could be there with her.

'Are we friends again then, or what?'

'Maybe we should be strangers. You said strangers would give each other more.'

'OK, let's be strangers again.'

'I'm looking forward to meeting you when you get home.'

'Stop sounding hurt.'

'You said I was useless with the kids. That hurt.'

'I didn't mean that.'

'You said it.'

'People say things they don't mean when they're angry.'

'Maybe it's true. Maybe I am.'

'Come on . . . It was just that I was making the dinner, and you should've been watching Lucy . . .'

'OK, OK, I know I should. But I was trying to talk to you, Madeleine. That's the whole problem . . . I mean, trying to be with each other . . . and the kids . . .'

He was unable to clarify the thought any further: as if on cue, Jenny cried out.

'Was that Lucy?'

'I think it was Jenny.'

'You better go to her. Jane's probably waiting for me at the bar.'

They said goodbye in a way that suggested a pact.

He put the phone down and went into the hall, where Jenny stood rubbing her eyes and squinting up at him. He crouched down beside her and took her in his arms.

'What's the matter – did something wake you up?'

'Who were you talking to on the phone, Dad?'

'Nobody.'

'It must have been somebody.'

'Back to bed now, eh?'

'Was it a stranger?'

'Well yes, it was.'

'You shouldn't talk to strangers, Dad. Unless you're with me or Lucy, then it's OK to talk to a stranger.'

He looked at her and grinned.

'Is that right?'

She nodded, pleased with her own formulation of the situation. She elaborated it:

'If you've got a kid or a toddler or even if you've got a baby with you, it's OK to talk to a stranger.'

'I'll remember that.'

'But not if you're on your own, Dad. Sometimes people are strangerous.'

'You mean dangerous?'

'Dangerous *and* strangerous. Where's Mum?'

'Out.'

'When is she coming back?'

'Not for a while yet. You go back to bed now, eh?'

'Can I have a drink? I'm getting a bit dehydrated.'

She had picked up the word from Miss Horner, who had apparently told the dance class about the dangers of perspiration and the need to replace bodily fluids.

He got her a glass of milk, waited until she drank it, took her back to her room and settled her down in bed. He talked about painting her room and asked her what colour she'd like – pink, with silver stripes and gold polka dots – then went back to the kitchen.

It had grown dark in the room, in the house, and soon he found himself moving from room to room, switching on the lights as he went. In the living room he switched on the TV. He didn't want to watch it, but wanted the background noise of it and the moving coloured light. There were two small lights as well as the overhead light. He switched these on too, before leaving the room. Finally he returned to the bedroom, but when he switched on the bedside lamp he changed his mind and switched it off again. He lay down on the bed. The light from the hall shone in through the half-open door and he could hear the low monologue of the TV news in the living room.

He was impatient to see her. She would be herself with him again, and he with her. At least, they would be strangers of a kind again, and they would talk as only strangers are free to. And there was so much he needed to tell her, now that they were speaking to each other again. So much had happened to him in the last few days that he'd kept from her – kept, in a way, from himself. So he lay, going over the ordinary events of his day – helping Lucy up the climbing frame, holding her as she hung from the rings, the argument with Madeleine, talking to Jenny about Miss Horner and her dehydration, that Peruvian woman, that smile! – all these things crowded into his mind and appeared to him utterly new and astonishing, until his own life seemed like another life he was watching from a distance, or reading about in a book, a life that seemed valuable, seemed meaningful . . . And although he was utterly alone, he was still in a dark room with a stranger.